The Bible Club Mysteries 1

I0547455

The Case of the Ten-Thousand Dollar Gumball

Ryan Hobbs

Delaware
Spring Press

This book is a work of fiction. Any similarities regarding people, living or dead, or events is coincidental.

Unless otherwise identified, all Scripture quotations in this publication are taken from the Holy Bible: New International Version®, NIV® Copyright © 1973, 1978, 1984 by International Bible Society. Used by permission of Zondervan Publishing House. All rights reserved worldwide.

ISBN: 978-0-9838092-7-2

To Evan, Drew, and Katie:

The Inspiration for the Bible Club

Chapter One

"Bang. Bang," said the little, freckle-faced cowboy as he shot his plaster six-shooters. "Mommy, I got the bad guy."

"Please Alex, give me a minute," his mother replied without turning away from the balding, heavy-set man behind the counter. "The medicine can't be that much. It wasn't that much last month. We can't afford it."

"I'm sorry Mrs. Townsend," Mr. Gruber said apologetically, "the prices on most of my medications just keep rising. There isn't anything I can do."

Alex pointed his gun at Mr. Gruber.

"Put your hands up!"

A gentle smile came across the pharmacist's chubby cheeks as he did as he was told.

"Not now, Alex," Mrs. Townsend scolded the boy. "But my husband has to have this," she said, resuming her previous conversation.

"Are you close to having enough?" asked Mr. Gruber.

Mrs. Townsend fumbled through her purse searching for her money.

Meanwhile, Alex had begun running about the store, guns blazing. No desperados were safe from the little hero. First, he took aim at Mr. Owens, the banker, who was searching for his familiar brand of antacid. Next, he fired two shots at little-old Ethel Stoltzfus, who was shopping the candy aisle for the little peppermints she always gave out to the children at church. (Ethel was very deaf, and nearly blind, so she took no notice of Alex.) Then, he spied the magazine rack by the front door. From the cover of a well-known sport's journal, a famous baseball player stared the boy down. Alex returned the stare as he placed his guns back into their holsters. A second later, he cried "draw" and pulled out his guns, firing a dozen shots at the cover.

The Yankee's shortstop didn't stand a chance.

Still scouring through her purse, Alex's mom had grown visibly flustered. "I know I had more money than this," she muttered. "It must be here somewhere."

As his mother continued to search, the cowboy decided that thieves were headed down the alley with stolen loot. Hoping to head them off at the pass, Alex tore away towards the back door, his oversized boots thumping against the store's faded hardwood flooring. Unfortunately, the boy went out the rear exit just as Mr. Farmer came in it. The two collided. Mr. Farmer, whose occupation just happened to match his name, was surprised but unharmed. However, the cowboy landed hard upon his britches. With a steely eyed gaze, the boy climbed to his feet, aiming his revolvers at his newest rival.

"Stick 'em up, Mister!" Alex cried.

Hearing the commotion, Mrs. Townsend looked up.

"Alexander Jonathan Townsend," she snapped, "can't you stay out of trouble for a moment? Go wait out front until I'm done!" Turning back to Mr. Gruber, she apologized. Then, after a nervous pause, she added, "It looks like…it looks like…I only have half the money." Unable to hold it back any longer, Mrs. Townsend erupted into a fountain of tears.

While Mr. Gruber handed a tissue to the overwhelmed mother, young Alex pouted and stomped his way out the front of the store.

There, still feeling the sting of his mother's anger, Alex threw himself on a bench beneath the shop window. His long face hidden underneath his drooping ten-gallon hat, the boy sat motionless. But after several long minutes, without anyone to feel sorry for him, Alex gave up on his sullenness. Instead, he picked his head up and began to take in his surroundings.

The first thing that caught his eye was a gumball machine sitting in the store's entryway. He hopped up and walked over, greedily eying the extra-large rainbow-colored treats. He was penniless, however. So Alex turned to wishful thinking. But a twisting of the machine's handle and a lifting of the chute's door soon gave him a harsh lesson in reality—no coin, no gumball. Disappointed, yet still waiting on his mother's return, the boy, once again, felt the call of the Old West.

Crouching behind the bench, Alex began shooting each passersby with his plastic revolvers. Still, no mother. Next, he pretended the bench was a wild stallion which only the fearless cowboy could tame. Still, no mother. Then, he began jumping down from the top of the bench, imagining that the cowboy was leaping from the back of a flaming stagecoach. And, still, no mother. Soon, Alex's games began taking him further and further down Main Street. Until finally, he was running and bounding and shooting everything within two blocks, north or south, of the little pharmacy.

Eventually, the cowboy's adventures led him to the front of the dry cleaners. There, suddenly, the boy lowered his guns. Alex had spotted something. He had spotted something shiny. It was laying in the middle of the sidewalk.

He pounced like a cat.

After scooping it up and examining it, the boy discovered that he had a nickel, or did he? Certainly it was a coin, and it was about the size of a nickel. But Alex knew that nickels were silver and this was gold. And there was something wrong with the face too. At six-years-old, Alex didn't know to expect Thomas Jefferson's image. However, he did find the man on the coin to be somewhat funny and unfamiliar. Why did the man have leaves in his hair? And wasn't there supposed to be a lot of words? This coin only said *T-I-C-A-E-S-A-R-D-I-V-I* on the front and *P-O-N-T-I-F* on the back, whatever those letters meant.

Although he was curious about his find, a more powerful thought quickly overtook him. With the coin in hand, Alex raced back to the front of the pharmacy.

"It fits," he exclaimed joyfully, after placing the coin in the gumball machine.

He turned the knob and heard the marvelous sound of a gumball falling into the chute. Then, after a grab and a gobble, the boy began chomping away at his enormous yellow delight.

When his mother finally emerged from the store, carrying the prized medicine as well as a few small grocery items, Alex was sitting on the bench happily working his bubble gum.

"There you are," she said, no longer showing any signs of her earlier tears. "Sorry it took so long. Mrs. Stoltzfus saw me and began telling me all about her cats. I know more about Mr. Whiskers and his friends than anyone would care to know. Anyway, would you believe that Mr. Gruber *gave me* Daddy's medicine *and* these groceries? I just can't believe it. He was so kind." She took Alex's hand and began to walk down the sidewalk. "I don't know what we are going to do when Daddy needs his refill next month, but…what are you chewing on?"

"A giant gumball," mumbled the boy happily.

"A gumball?" his mother answered. "Where did you get the money for a gumball?"

"I found a nickel on the sidewalk."

"Well, aren't you a lucky cowboy," she said with a grin.

Several evenings later, a weary Mr. Gruber pulled the pharmacy door closed, put in his key, and turned it quickly to the left. After checking the handle to make sure that it was locked, he swung around to begin his walk home. Upon turning, however, his eyes quickly settled on the gumball machine. "Oh, that foolish thing," he sighed, his head and shoulders drooping. For days, one child after another had complained that the handle was stuck. He had meant to take a look at it but kept putting it off.

"Alright," he grumbled, apparently speaking to the gumball machine, "I'll fix you."

With one last sigh, he turned back around, unlocked the door, and disappeared inside.

A few moments later, Mr. Gruber reappeared with a flashlight, a screwdriver, and an oddly shaped, red-handled key. Bending over the machine, the pharmacist tried the handle. It was indeed stuck. "This always happens to you when the kids put Canadian nickels in your mouth," he said, still speaking to the gumball machine. Lowering his large body down upon his knees, Mr. Gruber inserted the red-handled key into the machine's back and opened the coin depository. Then he removed the coin tray. Using his left hand, he turned on his flashlight and aimed the beam into the newly formed opening. With his right, he pushed in the screwdriver and began poking it upward. After a number of thrusts, he pulled the screwdriver back out and attempted to turn the handle. No luck, it wouldn't turn. So he tried the procedure over again. And, still no luck.

In fact, it wasn't until the fifth try that Mr. Gruber successfully turned the handle. By this time, however, the pharmacist was much too tired and hungry to care about the coin that tumbled out of the machine and onto the sidewalk. Instead, grumbling about his dinner being cold, Mr. Gruber quickly put the gumball machine back together and returned his tools to the store. Once more he locked the front door and turned to leave. But then, after taking the first two steps toward home, Mr. Gruber suddenly stopped. There had been something peculiar about that coin which he dislodged, and the thought wouldn't go away.

He slowly turned around.

With the only light coming from a dim streetlamp, the pharmacist had to squint to search the ground. But it didn't take him long. There was the coin, laying at the edge of the sidewalk, a few feet away from the entrance to his store.

With a strange look upon his face, Mr. Gruber bent over and retrieved the coin. He lifted it up to his eye and then froze.

"Oh my…," he whispered in astonishment.

After staring, open mouthed, for an entire minute, a burst of excitement overcame him. He took a step toward the store but decided better of it. He looked up and down the street, searching for someone to tell. There was no one around. "What do I do?" he said to himself, clasping the coin tightly in his hand. He took several steps in the direction of home. Then, once again, he stopped.

"What am I doing?" he thought. "I need to concentrate. First of all, is this what I think it is?" He took a deep breathe. "It can't be real. But I have to find out. Where did I see this before? The coin auction guide? No, no, it wasn't there. I was looking in that coin collecting magazine. Where did I get that? Was it the library?" He took another deep breathe. "Slow down, Bill. Yes, of course, it was the library." Mr. Gruber checked his watch. "They don't close for fifteen minutes. I can still make it."

With his course of action now set, Mr. Gruber hustled off.

It was nine-o-five exactly when Chief's home phone rang.

"Hello," answered the sleepy police chief.

"Chief, this is Bill Gruber," said the excited voice coming through the receiver. "I've found something that you've got to see...."

Chapter Two

"Come on," Abigail said, tucking her legs beneath her on the saggy green sofa, "let's get started."

"Yeah, let's go," Miles seconded impatiently, as he rolled his wheelchair into its typical spot by the bookshelf.

Slowly and with a great deal of commotion, the others made their way over, each sitting in their familiar spot. Declan next to Grant on the worn, gray folding chairs. Talia beside Abigail on the couch. Grace, Abigail's little sister, between the couch and Miles, half-swallowed by an over-sized bean bag. And Tomas, seated on the floor to the left of Chief's cracked-leather recliner, completing the circle. The only spot remaining belonged to Zayne. His wooden desk chair, always positioned on Chief's right, sat empty. However, all of the members of the Bible club had learned never to expect it to be filled on time.

With a warm smile upon his face, Chief waited patiently for his young friends to settle in and to open their Bibles. "Let's pray," he said finally. Then he proceeded to ask God to be with them as they prepared to study from God's Word.

Chief was a white-haired man of medium height and modest build. And although nearing seventy, he still looked healthy and fit. Despite the appearance, however, his forty-five years on the police force had taken their toll. The aches and pains of severe arthritis, not to mention his recent knee surgery, had slowed him considerably.

Of course, Chief wasn't his real name. But after spending twenty years leading the city's police department, no one called him anything else. To everyone, he was Chief, plain and simple. To everyone, that was, except the group of youngsters who sat around his living room week after week. For each of the members of the

Bible Club, the kind and humble old lawman could also be called mentor, teacher, and friend.

"Today," Chief began, "I want us to examine one of my favorite things about Jesus. I want us to study his brilliance. Considering his humble upbringing, it is another of his characteristics that makes him truly unique. And to be quite honest, it played a very important role in my decision to become a Christian." Chief paused and reached for his coffee cup on the end table. As he did so, it caused him to twist his right knee ever so slightly. A grimace of pain came to Chief's face. Despite a month passing since his surgery, the knee still needed to be treated gingerly. "Turn to Matthew chapter twenty-two and let's start reading in verse fifteen," he added after the pain had subsided. "Talia would you begin?"

"I'd be delighted," she replied in her typically proper way. The twelve-year-old, Indian-born girl had spent most of her childhood living in Great Britain. Her mannerisms and speech reflected it.

Talia looked down at the Bible in her lap. Immediately, strands of her long, thick black hair engulfed the book. "Then the Pharisees went out and laid plans to trap him in his words," she read, holding the pesky hair back as she did so. "They sent their disciples to him along with the Herodians."

"Who are the Fairy Bees and the Hero Indians?" asked seven-year-old Grace.

The others chuckled.

"That's a very good question, Grace," Chief replied, unable to suppress a smile. "Does anyone remember?"

Declan, the only son of a pastor, spoke up. "The Pharisees are Jesus' main enemies. They tried really hard to follow God, but all of their trying had turned into lots and lots of rules," he explained. For thirteen, Declan knew a great deal about the Bible. "And

10

somewhere in all those rules," he continued, "they had forgotten how to love God. But I don't think I can explain about the Herodians. I remember the name, yet that's about it."

Twelve-year-old Miles raised his strong right arm to speak. Having been in a wheelchair since he was very young, Miles rolled himself everywhere. He would have been the Bible Club's arm wrestling champion if not for his new friend Grant, who at thirteen had the size and strength of a grown man.

"If I remember correctly. Herod ruled Galilee, where Jesus was from," Miles began after Chief had called on him. "So, I bet Herodians were his followers."

"That's right Miles," Chief answered. "Israel, the country where Jesus and the rest of the Jewish people lived, had been taken over by the Roman Empire. They had a Roman born ruler over part of the country, but Herod was a Jew that the Romans had placed in charge of the other part. People think that the Herodians were a political group friendly toward Herod. Keep going Talia."

"Teacher," they said, "we know that you are a man of integrity and that you teach the way of God in accordance with the truth. You aren't swayed by others, because you pay no attention to who they are."

"Give me a break," Tomas exclaimed with a hint of the Spanish accent that only appeared when he got excited. "They are laying it on pretty thick, aren't they? We know how awesome you are, and how you *only* teach what's right. Blah, blah, blah. Jesus isn't going to fall for their brown-nosing."

"What's brown-nosing?" Grace asked as she inadvertently rubbed the end of her nose.

While Grace spoke, her big sister Abigail, who had celebrated her thirteenth birthday days before, sat listening. As usual, the older sibling had a pink ink pen thrust through the right side of her brown hair and resting upon her ear. Like a knight drawing a sword, Abigail pulled the pen out and pointed it directly at Grace. "Do you remember how you kept saying all of those nice things about me last week," Abigail said, "just so that I would let you be at my birthday party?"

"Yeah."

"That's brown-nosing."

"So the Fairy Bees and the Hero Indians wanted Jesus to invite them to his birthday party!" Grace declared with a look of deep confusion.

"No Grace," said Declan kindly, "they were trying to get on Jesus' good side, just like you were with Abigail. But it wasn't because of a party. They wanted to flatter Jesus, hoping he'd get a big head and not realize that they were trying to catch him in a trap. Am I right Chief?"

"Exactly," Chief answered. "Read the next verse Talia. Listen carefully everyone, and see if you can understand why it's a trap."

"Tell us then, what is your opinion? Is it right to pay the imperial tax to Caesar or not?"

"I think I see it," Abigail said excitedly as she unfolded her legs from beneath her and sat up straight on the couch. "Everybody had to pay their taxes. So if Jesus said that people didn't have too, he'd be in big trouble."

"That makes sense," replied Tomas, who had been taking notes. Although unusual for a twelve-year-old boy, Tomas was extremely organized.

"Well, if Jesus will get in trouble, why doesn't he just tell them to pay?" Grant asked in his unnaturally deep voice.

For a moment, the group was startled into silence. In part, because they didn't have an answer to the question. But mostly because Grant was painfully shy and rarely spoke.

"That's a great question, Grant," said Chief warmly. "Why doesn't Jesus just tell everyone to pay their taxes?"

As if the thought slipped out by accident, Miles quietly said, "I guess because everyone hates paying taxes."

"Quite right," Talia added. "And remember, since Israel has been taken over by the Romans, the Jewish people are being asked to pay taxes to someone they despise."

"So," Abigail exclaimed, "if Jesus says, 'don't pay taxes,' then the Roman government is going to come after him. But, if Jesus says, 'pay your taxes,' he is going to turn the people against him because they don't want to pay the taxes."

"I get it," said Tomas, "Jesus is trapped. There's no way to answer the question without getting in big time trouble."

"Nasty trick," Miles said, shaking his head slowly. "Nasty, nasty trick."

"So, what does he do?" Grant asked, already having spoken more during this meeting than in the last three combined.

"Keep reading," Chief answered, delighted that the study had captured their attention.

"Oh, please let me read," little Grace begged.

After Talia smiled and nodded, Grace began, "But Jesus, knowing their evil in…in…in…"

"Intent," Talia helped, "that means *what they were really up to.*"

"…evil intent," resumed Grace, "said, 'you hypo'…hippos…why are there hippos in this story?"

"Hypocrites," corrected Declan patiently. "That means they are phonies."

"'… *hypocrites*," Grace continued, pronouncing the word very slowly, "why are you trying to trap me? Show me the coin used for paying the tax.' They brought him a…," Grace put her hands on her hips and gave an exasperated look.

Chief came to her rescue, "Denarius. It was a coin. Think of it like a quarter or a dime."

"Why didn't they just say quarter or dime," Grace proclaimed with considerable attitude. "It would make more sense." Several people laughed. Grace read on. "They brought him a denarius, and he asked them, 'Whose image is this? And whose inscription?' 'Caesar's,' they replied. Then he said to them, 'So give back to Caesar what is Caesar's, and to God what is God's.' When they heard this, they were amazed. So they left him and went away."

"Smashing," Talia declared.

"Awesome," Miles and Abigail said in unison.

"I don't get it," Tomas humbly admitted.

Declan came to Tomas' aide.

"He found a way out when there was no way out," he said excitedly. A sparkle of delight in his big blue eyes.

"Don't you see?" Declan asked rhetorically. "It was Caesar's picture on the money. Okay, then give it to him. He made it. Let him have it. So Jesus is saying, in the cleverest way possible, to pay the tax. It's the Roman's money anyway. But at the same time, he says, 'give to God what is God's.'" Everyone listened intently as Declan continued. "And Jesus teaches the people a big spiritual lesson. God doesn't care about stuff. He wants people's hearts, and that is what the Jews are to give to God. Amazing. Jesus escapes the trap perfectly. He won't get in trouble with the Roman's and the people aren't angry with him. All of this while giving the people what they want and need the most—the truth about God."

"Now I get it," Tomas said with a smile. "I love how it ends, 'they were amazed. So they left him and went away.' They thought they were so clever, but they were the ones who didn't know what to say. Nice!"

Just then, the noise of a door could be heard swinging open and then banging closed. Loud awkward steps made their way down the hallway. Suddenly, a wild-eyed eleven-year-old with unkempt red hair and a face covered with freckles, stumbled into the room.

"Am I late?" Zayne asked absently.

"No, you aren't late," Abigail noted. "Technically, you are absent, because we just finished the study. Where were you?"

"I had a terrible run-in with a hamster," Zayne said, revealing an enormous unravelling bandage upon his left thumb.

"A hamster," Declan said in disbelief, "did you get bitten?"

"Yeah," Zayne replied as he walked over to the pass through counter where Chief placed the refreshments. He helped himself to several enormous handfuls of cheese puffs. "I guess he got mad when I tried to put the saddle on him."

"A saddle?" everyone exclaimed.

"Why were you putting a saddle on a hamster?" Miles asked incredulously.

"It was an experiment," Zayne answered as he chomped on his cheese puffs. "I wanted to see if the mouse and the hamster could develop a symbiotic relationship..." Chomp. Chomp. "...sort of a friendship, you know."

"You were going to have a mouse ride on the back of a hamster," Talia laughed. Her laughter suddenly stopped. "Wait," she added, "you don't have a hamster."

"Yeah," Zayne acknowledged with a mouth full of puffs, "I didn't have a mouse either." Chomp. "…had to borrow the money from this big mean kid named Dirk. He said he would punch me in the face if I didn't pay him back with interest." Chomp. Chomp. Chomp. "Luckily, the pet store has a three day return policy. I think they do that just in case the animals keep going to the bathroom on the carpet and your parents get sick of it and won't let you keep them." Chomp. "I thought three days would give me just enough time to try my experiment, return the hamster and the mouse, and pay back Dirk." He began to pour himself a glass of soda. "The mouse wasn't too expensive, but you wouldn't believe what they charge for a hamster. It's outrageous! Do you think they'll still take them both back? You know, like how you can't return a pair of sneakers if you get them dirty. The hamster and the mouse are, sort of, well, they are kind of, um, angrier than they were when I got them."

Zayne took a loud slurp of his soda.

"By the way, could someone lend me ten dollars?" he asked, an orange mustache now appearing over his upper lip. "That's the amount of interest that I owe Dirk."

No one answered him. Instead, everyone just stared in disbelief.

"Come sit down Zayne," Chief said politely, pointing to Zayne's familiar chair beside him, "I've got a story I want to tell you."

"Yeah," Grace cheered.

"How delightful," Talia exclaimed. "One of your police stories, I hope."

"Please tell us one of your police stories," Abigail begged. "They really are so much fun to listen to. Is it a police story?"

"Do I have any other kind?" Chief laughed.

"What's it about Chief?" Miles asked excitedly.

"Well, it's kind of an odd story," Chief began, "and to tell you the truth, the only time I ever think of it is when I read the passage that we studied today. It happened twenty years ago. Late one evening, as I had just begun preparing for bed, I got a call from Bill Gruber. Bill's an old friend of mine. He runs that pharmacy down on Main Street. Anyway, he asked me if it would be okay if he dropped by my house. He said that he had found something and that he wanted me to take a look it. 'What was it?' I asked. 'Well,' he said, 'somebody just paid ten-thousand dollars for a gumball.'"

Chapter Three

"It was a *real* Roman coin?" Abigail asked.

"Completely authentic," Chief replied, setting his Bible on the end table. "In fact, Emperor Tiberius Caesar's picture had been engraved upon it. In all likelihood, Tiberius ruled the Roman Empire when the Pharisees and the Herodians asked Jesus about paying the temple tax."

"You mean that they showed Jesus a coin with Tiberius' face?" Miles wondered.

"Probably," Chief said simply.

"Cool," Grant whispered, adding to his record word count.

"That's neat," offered Declan, his folding chair squeaking as he leaned forward. "I wonder if the coin in the gumball machine could have been the same one Jesus touched."

"Unlikely," Zayne interjected, having now taken his normal place beside Chief. "I'd estimate the odds of that to be...." He paused. Using a cheese puff as a pointer, Zayne appeared to be calculating a math problem in the air. "...about five hundred million to one," he finally decided, "give or take a few hundred thousand."

Satisfied with his calculations, the red-headed boy gobbled his pointer.

As Zayne chewed, however, Tomas fixated on the millions of tiny bits of bright orange powder that covered his friend's hands and mouth.

Unable to cope with the thought of cheese all over Chief's furniture, Tomas got up, went over to the refreshment counter, and picked up a napkin.

"Chief, did the owner of the coin ever come to claim it?" Tomas asked, throwing the napkin at Zayne as he dropped himself back into his spot on the floor. "Wipe your hands," he added in a forceful whisper, glaring at Zayne. "You're making a mess."

The napkin landed perfectly upon his friend's lap. However, rather than using it to wipe off the powder, Zayne left the napkin untouched, choosing instead to lick his fingers clean—one by one.

After each lick, Zayne smiled with delight.

Tomas sighed.

"No, they never did," answered Chief, ignoring Zayne's antics. "But we did figure out who put the coin into the gumball machine. It was a young boy named Alex Townsend. He found the coin on the sidewalk and thought it was a nickel."

"Amazing!" Miles declared. "He put an authentic Roman coin into a gumball machine."

"Wow, a coin worth ten-thousand pounds used to buy a five cent piece of candy," Talia marveled, not realizing she had mistakenly used British currency.

"You mean dollars," Miles corrected her with a wink.

"Oh yes, of course," Talia replied apologetically. "Ten-thousand *dollars*."

"Ef poundz," Zayne garbled, trying to both speak and lick the cheese from around his mouth at the same time, "ef woof ve bun werf eighf fouzan too, and ifty pounce."

"What?" Abigail asked, squinting at Zayne.

The red-headed boy finished licking and put his tongue back in his mouth.

"Sorry, I was trying to get the cheese off my face," Zayne explained. "I said, in pounds the gumball would be worth eight thousand two, and fifty pence. At least, based on the last exchange rates that I saw." He took an enormous gulp of his soda before proceeding. "Did you know that the British used to have a half penny? What good would a half-penny be? And, strangely, it took four hundred eighty of them to make a single pound. Just imagine what five pounds in half-pennies would weigh? You'd have to carry them all around in a wheelbarrow."

Despite the strange looks from the group, Zayne continued.

"And besides, do you think the store would turn you away just because you were a half penny short? I'm sorry, Governor," Zayne said, assuming a horrible British accent, "we cannot sell you these knickers. You'll need to come back when you find a half penny."

Grace stared at Zayne, her mouth slightly open.

"I have no idea what you are talking about," she said emphatically.

Everyone laughed good-naturedly.

Declan got up from his chair, went over to the refreshments, and picked up a serving bowl filled with pretzels. "Anybody want anything?" he asked. No one did. "Where's the coin now?" Declan asked Chief as he returned to his seat and placed the bowl of pretzels on his lap.

"Have you ever heard of Jess Evers?"

"Sure, Chief," Abigail replied. "He's that old television actor who grew up here. I've watched all the reruns of *The Hollywood Hayseeds.*"

"Oh, I love that show," Tomas exclaimed. "He's a poor country farmer who suddenly inherits millions and millions of dollars.

Makes me laugh every time I see it. Doesn't he live on the edge of town?"

"That's right, Tomas, he does," acknowledged Chief. "Evers has the coin now. Having retired from show business shortly before all of this happened, he moved back home. The story goes that he wanted to get away from the spotlight. Anyway, Evers is a big coin collector. He bought our mysterious Roman coin at auction." Chief paused, picked his coffee up off the end table, and took another drink.

"You see," Chief resumed, "since no one ever claimed it, the coin went back to the person who had found it. Truthfully, Bill Gruber should have been the rightful owner, but he's a kind-hearted Christian man." He paused once more to finish off what remained of the coffee. "And Bill let the boy have it."

"Alex Townsend?" asked Abigail, trying to make sure that she got all the facts straight.

"Right," answered Chief.

"And Alex put it up for auction?" Talia inquired.

"Well, his family did. Not right away, mind you. I think it was four or five years later if I recall correctly. Apparently times were tough for the family. They really needed the money."

"What I want to know," began Miles, tapping his right index finger upon the armrest of his wheelchair, "is how a Roman coin worth ten-thousand dollars ended up on Main Street in the first place?"

"Perhaps someone still using it as currency simply dropped it," replied Zayne in complete earnest.

"Zayne," Declan reminded him, "anyone still using a Roman coin as currency would have to be two-thousand years old."

"Actually," Zayne responded, sounding like a school teacher, "the eastern Roman Empire continued until 1453 A.D. So, a Roman need only be a little over five hundred years old. But that's not what I mean. I've seen several accounts that suggest Roman coins may have still been in use throughout parts of Europe as late as the nineteenth century."

"How do you know things like that?" asked Miles. "Do you read the encyclopedia?"

"Sometimes," acknowledged Zayne. "Anyway, although the odds are remote, there is a slight possibility that someone thought the coin was still in circulation."

"Don't you think that's a little far-fetched?" groaned Abigail.

"Yes, it is," Zayne conceded. "But if you are trying to solve a mystery, you must be careful not to rule out any possibility without first considering it."

"You're right, Zayne," Grace sneered while crossing her arms and tossing her head to one side. "We must never rule anything out. That's why *I* think it was dropped by a mouse riding on the back of a hamster."

"Grace," Zayne replied, having completely missed her sarcasm, "I didn't say that you can't rule some things out. A mouse would not have been able to carry a coin of that size and weight. And since that is not truly a possibility, it should be ruled out."

"You are not right, Zayne," Grace said, throwing her arms up in disbelief, "not right, at all."

"Miles, that was the key question for us too." Chief said, intending to refocus the conversation. "How did the coin end up on Main Street in the first place?" Before continuing, he gently released the lever on the side of his lounger. A pained expression came to the old policeman's face as the descending footrest caused his surgically

23

repaired knee to slowly bend. When both his feet were resting on the carpet and the pain had passed, Chief leaned forward.

"The most obvious explanation," he suggested, preparing to rise, "is that someone obtained the coin somewhere, perhaps from a collector in their family, and they simply didn't realize what they had. Then they carelessly lost it on the street."

"That is the most obvious explanation," Abigail remarked with a skeptical look on her face, "but that isn't what you believe, is it?"

"You're a clever girl, Abigail," Chief said, proud of his young friend.

With the help of a cane, Chief got up from his chair and slowly carried his cup over to the refreshment counter. There he poured himself some fresh coffee from a pot simmering on a hot plate. Meanwhile, the others waited in suspense. When Chief had added two sugars and some milk to his cup, yet still hadn't explained how he thought the coin got on the street, Miles could no longer maintain his silence.

"Chief," he begged with his hands on top of his head, "you're killing me. Aren't you going to tell us what you think happened?"

Leaving his cane resting against a wall, Chief limped his way back to his lounge chair, trying hard not to spill his fresh coffee. Handing the cup to Tomas, he carefully lowered himself back into the recliner. Then, once he was comfortable, Chief took the coffee back from Tomas and took a sip. He still had not spoken. As everyone continued to wait, they each began to realize that Chief was holding an inner debate. Should he or should he not tell them more about the case. Finally, he made up his mind.

"Okay," Chief said slowly. "I'll tell you what I think. But it's a bit tricky. So let's keep this to ourselves, alright?" He looked around the room at each of them, invoking such responses as "sure," "absolutely," and "I promise."

"According to what the little boy said," Chief began in a quiet, serious voice, "the coin was found in front of the dry cleaners on Main Street. So what does that matter? Well, for some time we had suspected Frank Miller, the owner of the dry cleaners, of fencing stolen coins."

"Did he put the fence around the coins?" a confused Grace wondered in an inappropriately loud voice.

"No Grace," Talia explained, "not that kind of fence. Fencing means that after something has been nicked...I mean stolen...someone buys the stuff from the crook. Later, they resell it."

"That's right," Chief continued, "the fencer serves as a middle-man between the thief and a buyer, providing a way for the thief to get money for the stolen goods. And, of course, the fencer sells the items for more than he paid the thief, allowing for a nice profit."

"Does that mean that the new buyer knows the stuff is stolen?" asked Declan.

"Sometimes they do," Chief explained, "and sometimes they don't. It kind of depends on how reputable the fence may appear to be. In the case of Miller, we suspect that he was selling to high end private collectors who knew the goods were probably stolen but who didn't care. So, we have rumors about Frank Miller the coin fence and we have an extremely valuable coin laying on the sidewalk, directly in front of his store. Doesn't that seem to be a rather unlikely coincidence?"

"I sure think so," said Abigail, biting on the end of her pink pen.

"But we could never find any evidence that the coin found in the gumball machine had been stolen," added Chief. "And despite lots of circumstantial evidence that Miller was, in fact, a key player in the regional stolen coin market, we were never able to catch him in the act of buying or selling anything. We had even tried an undercover sting, but he didn't bite."

"What do bees have to do with this?" Grace puzzled. "Now, I suppose you're going to say that it wasn't that kind of sting."

"It wasn't that kind of sting," the entire room answered in unison—except Grant.

"Grace, a sting is when the police try to trick the bad guy into committing a crime," explained Declan. "First, they have a policeman go undercover, which means they pretend to be someone they aren't. Second, they try to gain the trust of the bad guy. Finally, they offer the bad guy something illegal. If the bad guy takes it then that shows the police that he's a criminal. Chief, I guess you were probably trying to get Mr. Miller to buy a stolen coin?"

"We tried to get him to sell us one. But somehow he figured out what we were up to, and we didn't get anywhere. We kept an eye on him for years, but he was too careful. By the time I retired, I think Miller went legit. I don't think he has anything to do with stolen coins now. However, he still runs that same dry cleaners down on Main, and that's why I don't want you guys spreading this around."

"We understand," Talia replied while everyone nodded in agreement.

For the next hour or so, all the kids hung out at Chief's place. Tomas, Miles, and Grant played ping-pong on a table that Chief had set up in the garage. Talia challenged Zayne to some chess. Chief, whose hobby was photographing flowers, showed Declan and Abigail some old pictures he had taken. And Grace did a bit of this and that before leaving early to run over to her best friend Katie's. Mostly though, everyone ate and talked and laughed.

When it was finally time to head home, the members of the Bible Club all went as one, as they usually did. Together, side by side, they continued talking and laughing while the sun began to grow orange and pink over the horizon. As they worked their way up a hill, it was Miles, whose chair was being pushed by Grant up the steep incline, who brought the conversation back to the ten thousand dollar gumball.

"That was an interesting story about that Roman coin," he began. "I wonder if the coin really had been stolen."

"And if Mr. Miller had something to do with it," added Talia.

"I'd sure like to know what happened," said Abigail as she shifted her large study Bible from beneath her right arm to her left.

"Me too," agreed Tomas, whose short legs were working hard to keep up with his much taller friends. "But it was twenty-years ago. I guess if the coin was stolen whoever took it got away with it."

"You know," Declan said thoughtfully, "if the coin was stolen that might explain why no one claimed it. Certainly Mr. Miller wouldn't have claimed the coin if he was trying to fence it. And if there was a coin thief out there, he couldn't…"

"…he or she…" corrected Abigail.

"Right, he or she," continued Declan, "couldn't just show up at the police department to claim it."

Zayne's hair flopped violently as he nodded in agreement.

"But what about the victim?" Tomas asked. "If the coin was stolen, why didn't they come and claim the coin?"

"Spot on," agreed Talia.

"Maybe the coin had been stolen somewhere else," Miles offered.

"Yeah," said Abigail. "Maybe it had been stolen someplace far away from here."

"That would explain why no one claimed the coin and why the police couldn't find a record of it being stolen," said Miles, once again rolling himself.

Grant nodded his approval.

"Well," began Declan as their walking slowed, "that could be the reason or it could simply be that the coin wasn't stolen at all. Maybe someone just lost it. If you lose something, you might not claim it for the simple reason that you don't know it's gone."

Abigail stopped and turned to face the others. "Of course, Declan might be right, but there is only one way to find out," she said, her brown eyes blazing. "We need to investigate."

"But we're just a bunch of kids, and all of this happened twenty years ago," Declan protested, yet it was too late. Like a dam breaching its walls, the Bible Club could no longer be stopped.

Realizing his objections were in vain, Declan looked up to the sky and said a short prayer.

"God, just where is all of this going to lead?"

Chapter Four

Grant looked at the clock on the nightstand and panicked.

He was late.

Saturday morning had arrived and he needed to meet Zayne, Abigail, and Miles at Mr. Gruber's pharmacy on Main Street. Grant hadn't forgotten. In fact, he had been awake since seven o'clock in anticipation. But as often happened, he had lost track of the time while reading a good book. Presently, *The Silver Chair* by C.S. Lewis had caused the distraction.

Grant loved to read, but few people knew that. Actually, few people knew Grant much at all.

Mistaking his shyness for a lack of intelligence, nearly everyone thought of him as a dumb jock. And they couldn't have been further from the truth. Certainly Grant was a top athlete, but his motivation for playing sports came more from the expectations of others than from his own passion. He much preferred intellectual pursuits to the glory of the athletic field.

As for his shyness, it was a problem, and Grant knew it. Yet he felt powerless to change.

In fact, over the years, try as he might, instead of growing more social Grant found himself becoming less. And now, he rarely spoke unless spoken too.

Although he himself probably couldn't explain why, Grant's silence came from three places: his personality, his father's career, and the pressure to perform.

God made Grant an introvert who preferred a quiet night at home over any social setting. This was simply Grant, and there was no crime in that. However, well before he had come along, his Dad had chosen a life in the army. With that choice came lots and lots and lots of relocation, for when Uncle Sam said you had to move then you had to move. Of course this meant that every time Grant made a friend, he would soon have to leave his friend behind. Somewhere around the fourth move, Grant stopped trying. It simply hurt too much. Finally, lots of well-intended people had taught Grant a very dangerous lesson.

It happened like this. When everyone saw Grant's remarkable athletic skills, they pushed him to win. Winning is fun, and winning is fine, but it comes with a danger. If the message becomes 'perform or else' a child's self-image can be wounded. The young person can come to believe that their value lies in their successes. Or put another way, they are loved only if they achieve. Naturally sensitive, Grant picked up on the underlying message, and the weight of its burden pushed him further inward.

Right before the school year, Grant's family moved yet again, this time into the same neighborhood as Miles. It was a very good thing.

From the first day they met, Miles went out of his way to befriend Grant. Miles always had a gift for connecting with people, especially those with whom others could not. But in the case of his relationship with Grant, Miles genuinely found it to be easy. For under the surface, the best athlete in the school and the boy in the wheelchair were really very much alike.

And so, it was growing increasingly true that if you were ever to look for one of them, you were bound to find the other.

This new friendship with Miles had already done a great many things for Grant, yet the most important thing of all had been an invitation to the Bible Club. Despite all of the teams he'd been on, before the Bible Club, Grant had never had a place where he felt like he belonged. (At least, he had never felt like he belonged simply for who he was and not for what he could do.) He looked forward to every meeting, and he had even used his own money to buy a Bible. In fact, Grant became the first person in his family to own one.

Grant loved his new friends, and he certainly didn't want to let them down. So he tossed his book upon his bed, smashed his feet into his already tied shoes, and raced down the hall. When he got to the stairs, Grant half flew, taking the flight three steps at a time.

After snatching a donut and a bottled water, he was out the door and into the garage.

Grant then dropped the water into his bicycle's bottle cage and quickly scarfed down the donut. Next, he threw his right leg over the top bar of his bike, and soon his long, thick legs were pumping down the driveway. Moments later, Grant had left his neighborhood far behind as he speed off toward downtown.

The Bible Club's first decision about their investigation had been to limit the number of people sent to interview Mr. Gruber. With such a large crowd, the interviewee might not feel comfortable. As a result, the friends had played rock-paper-scissors. The winners got to talk with Mr. Gruber. The losers would head to the library, doing research into the question of whether or not the coin had been stolen.

Abigail, Zayne, Grant, and Miles had won, turning Talia, Declan, and Tomas into the researchers. (Abigail invited her sister Grace to participate. But because of her age, their mom thought it would be best if she didn't. To put it mildly, Grace didn't agree.)

So as Grant peddled hard toward the pharmacy, the rest of his friends were also on the move. Everyone, that is, except Abigail and Zayne. In her typically responsible fashion, Abigail already stood outside of *Gruber's Hometown Pharmacy*. And, in his typically irresponsible fashion, Zayne remained in his bedroom, desperately searching for his left shoe.

Soon, Miles and Grant had joined Abigail at the pharmacy. No one bothered to mention Zayne being late. Instead, they began discussing their plan.

"So what's our goal here?" Abigail asked, trying to hide her excitement.

"Well," Miles began, "I think we simply want to ask him to tell us the story of finding the coin, from his perspective. That's what they do on the detective shows. Maybe he'll recall something that Chief didn't remember."

Grant nodded in agreement.

"Right," said Abigail, removing her pink pen and a small notebook from a drawstring bag she had tied to the handlebars of her bike. "Is that all?"

"I guess so," Miles answered.

"What if we also asked if he has any theories on how the coin ended up on the street?" added Abigail.

Miles and Grant both thought it was a good idea.

Abigail took a deep breath. "Well," she declared, "now that we are actually doing this, I'm nervous. But let's give it a go."

The three friends approached the entrance.

"Did I mention that I'm nervous?" Abigail repeated, hesitating in front of the door.

She took one last deep breath and then reached for the door handle.

As the handle turned, all three of the friends suddenly became aware of a strange thumping sound coming down the sidewalk. Turning to see, they were greeted by a ridiculous sight.

Running toward them was Zayne, wearing a pair of bright green galoshes. On each rain boot were two large yellow eyes and a bright red tongue. The rubber soles thudded and squeaked with each stride.

When he had joined them at the entrance to the pharmacy, a clearly tired Zayne bent over at the waist and put his hands upon his knees.

"What in the world are you wearing?" asked a stunned Abigail.

"What do you mean?" Zayne answered while trying to catch his breath.

"Uh...on your feet," Abigail said with a snicker.

Apparently having forgotten about his choice of footwear, Zayne looked down. "Oh, these are just my froggy boots. They were all I could find. I think I left one of my tennis shoes at Declan's house yesterday."

Normally if anyone made such a statement then the next question would be to ask how someone could leave behind a single shoe. However, with Zayne, none of the three friends bothered.

Instead, Miles wondered about another mystery. "Well, why didn't you ride your bike?" he inquired. "Your house must be nearly two miles away."

"I couldn't find it," Zayne said simply, having begun to breathe normally. "I think I might have left it over at your house," he added, pointing at Abigail.

A few moments later, the members of the Bible Club stood in front of the pharmacy counter, looking at a heavy-set man with graying hair.

"Can I help you kids with something?"

"Yes, sir," began Abigail, "a friend of ours told us about the time you found a rare coin in your gumball machine, and we wondered if you might have a few minutes to tell us more about it."

A look of confusion passed over the man's face. "A rare coin in the gumball machines…I don't think that I've ever…why, did you lose one?"

"Well, no, uh, we didn't," continued Abigail, caught off guard by his response. "Sir, aren't you William Gruber?"

"I am."

There was a moment of awkward silence as the four friends stared at each other in bewilderment. Had Chief been incorrect about the entire story? Had it never even happened? It was Zayne, however, who spoke next.

"Mr. Gruber," Zayne asked, rubbing his right hand through his wild red hair, "is there any chance you are William Gruber, Junior?"

"Ah, yes," the man behind the counter exclaimed, a broad smile erupting across his face, "that's it. I am William Gruber, Junior. You must want my Dad, William Gruber, Senior. But kids, he hasn't run the pharmacy in years. If someone lost a coin in the gumball machine, I would have been the one to find it, and I haven't found anything."

"It was quite some time ago, Sir," offered Miles. "Actually, twenty years ago."

The younger Mr. Grubber nodded. "Well, you're in luck. Dad's here now. He's supposed to be retired, but he still comes in for a few hours each day. Just go through that doorway at the back there," he said, pointing down the aisle filled with dental care products, "and you'll see him in the stock room."

The kids thanked the pharmacist, who gave them a final smile before turning his attention to another customer.

After walking down the aisle and passing through the rear doorway, Abigail, Miles, Grant and Zayne found themselves in a small rectangular room crammed with shelves and boxes. There, in a corner, with his back to them, sat an old man. Quite a hefty fellow, with a few thin strands of white hair combed neatly across the top of his otherwise bald head, the man sat upon an old stool. He was watching a fishing show on a small black and white television. The volume on the set had been raised extremely high.

"Excuse me, sir," Abigail interrupted, but there was no response.

She tried again, a bit louder this time. Still no answer.

"Tap him on the shoulder," Miles whispered to Abigail.

"You do it," Abigail answered.

"No way," replied Miles. They both looked at Grant, who simply shook his head.

Meanwhile as the others were arguing, Zayne had quietly walked over and sat down upon a large box beside Mr. Gruber, joining the old man in watching the fishing show.

"Have you ever caught a largemouth bass, son?" Mr. Gruber asked Zayne in a loud voice, not the least bit concerned that the boy had suddenly appeared in the stock room out of thin air.

"No, sir, I haven't."

"They put up a heck of a fight, I'll tell you. Give you quite a work out."

"Mr. Gruber, do you know the world record for a largemouth?" Zayne inquired without taking his eyes off the television.

"What's that? Speak up, son, my hearing aid is on the fritz."

"DO YOU KNOW THE WORLD RECORD FOR A LARGEMOUTH?"

"I'd guess about nineteen pounds. No, wait, maybe twenty. Yeah, I'll go with twenty pounds."

"Close," Zayne corrected, nearly yelling, "but not quite. It is actually twenty-two pounds and four ounces. Two men are tied for the record."

"Is that right?" the elder Mr. Gruber replied, shaking his head in disbelief.

Abigail, Miles, and Grant came forward and joined Zayne.

"Excuse me, sir," Abigail shouted, "would you mind if we asked you a couple questions about the time you found that Roman coin in the gumball machine?"

"Squeak in the pinball machine? Honey, I've never had a pinball machine in the pharmacy."

"No, sir, the Roman coin that you found in the gumball machine…twenty years ago."

Mr. Gruber turned to Zayne. "What is she saying?"

"We wondered about the coin you found," said Zayne simply.

"Oh yeah," Mr. Gruber answered, having apparently heard Zayne perfectly. "The Roman coin I found out front in the gumball machine. How'd you kids hear about that? It must have been twenty years ago." Seeing an opportunity to tell a story, something Mr.

Gruber loved to do, he got up from his stool and turned off the television. "I'll tell you all about it. But first, you kids need a soft drink."

A short time later, all of the investigators, along with Mr. Gruber, were settled around a small picnic table behind the store, each sipping on a bottle of red cream soda.

"Ah," Mr. Gruber said after taking a gulp from his drink, "there is something about the old style bottle that just makes the soda taste better. Now, you kids wanted to ask me about that coin. Shoot."

"Yes, sir," said Abigail, setting her nearly full cream soda down on top of the picnic table. "Our friend Chief told us about it, and we just wondered if you might recount what happened, in your own words." Although still speaking loudly, Abigail didn't need to shout. Since turning off the television, Mr. Gruber's ability to hear had improved considerably.

"Chief's a good man," began the old pharmacist. "We've been friends for years. Invited him to our men's Bible study, back in the day. He never misses. Still go fishing together too. How do you know Chief?"

"He leads our Bible Club," answered Zayne, who had already finished his drink and was greedily eyeing Abigail's.

"So why all of this interest in a coin I found way back when?"

"We just like a good mystery," Miles offered.

"That old policeman is discipling you in more ways than one," Mr. Gruber chuckled. "Alright, I'll tell you what I know, and maybe you kids can solve what we grown-ups never could."

For the next fifteen minutes, Mr. Gruber recounted, with great detail and excitement, how he found the Roman coin. Although entertaining, the story was essentially the same as what Chief had told them, offering the investigators nothing new.

When the old man had finished, Miles was the first to speak.

"Mr. Gruber, how did you know the coin was Roman?" he asked.

"Good question, son," Mr. Gruber answered with a nod. "Although my wife just calls me a pack rat, I'm a collector of this and that. I like old signs and old photographs. I have lots of old baseball cards and old stamps. And while I don't have much of a collection, I do have some rare coins, nothing terribly valuable mind you. If I had more money," the retired pharmacist said, patting a rear trouser pocket which contained his billfold, "I'd have more coins, I suppose. It's just a very expensive hobby. The pharmacy always made me a nice living, but I'm not rich."

Abigail, Miles, Grant, and Zayne smiled politely.

"Anyway," the old man continued, "I recognized the coin from a magazine I had recently looked through at the library. Although, I think I would have known anyway. The image was clearly either Greek or Roman, but the lettering pointed toward the later."

"Did you immediately recognized the worth of the coin?" asked Abigail, who had been recording Mr. Gruber's words in her notebook.

"Another good question," he replied, clearly enjoying the opportunity to talk. "Yes, knowing it to be Roman was easy. But knowing it to be valuable on the other hand, that wasn't. For just because a coin is old it doesn't necessarily mean that it's worth a lot of money. Some Roman coins are only appraised at a couple of hundred bucks, depending upon their condition. Yet this coin was mint, which is coin collector talk for perfect. And the one like it in the coin collecting magazine had sold at auction for ten thousand dollars. That's why, after going back to the library to double check, I called Chief. It isn't every day that someone loses something worth ten grand."

While Mr. Gruber spoke, Zayne had begun sticking one finger after another into the mouth of his empty soda bottle. Apparently he wanted to discover if any of his fingers were large enough to get stuck in the opening. When he had tried his thumb, Zayne found out the answer.

Without the slightest bit of concern, however, Zayne asked the retired pharmacist if he had any ideas about how the coin could have ended up on the sidewalk. As he waited on Mr. Gruber's reply, Zayne began pulling at the bottle.

"Twist the bottle while you pull," the old man suggested, "and it will come right out."

Zayne tried the suggestion and his thumb came free with a loud pop.

"Well," Mr. Gruber resumed, acting as if Zayne's behavior was not the least bit out of the ordinary, "if you want to know the truth, I do have a theory, which I told to the police at the time." Before continuing, he leaned forward and lowered his voice. "For over forty years, provided decent weather, this picnic table has been where I eat my lunch. And for years prior to finding that coin, I would occasionally see some, let's call them rough characters, entering the back of Frank Miller's dry cleaners. You see, if you look down the alley there," the old pharmacist said, pointing just past a blue dumpster, "that's the back of his place. Now, Frank is not really the nicest person you are ever going to meet. In fact, there is something, I don't know, shady about him. Anyway, it might have just been gossip, but one of my customers once told *me* that a friend of a friend of a friend had told *him* that Frank Miller was doing more than just cleaning shirts in that shop of his."

"What was he doing?" wondered Abigail, who hoped Mr. Gruber would confirm Chief's allegations that Frank Miller fenced stolen coins.

"Now, keep this quiet, okay?" Mr. Gruber said in an even quieter tone. "But my customer had heard that Miller was selling some kind of upscale stolen property."

He paused and looked both ways as if afraid someone might be listening.

"Of course, I don't know this for sure, but I wondered if that stolen property might just be stolen coins. Maybe Miller accidently dropped it on the sidewalk, or perhaps one of his mysterious visitors did."

"Did you happen to see any of those rough characters going into the back of Miller's store around the time you found the coin?" asked Miles, totally captivated by Mr. Gruber's idea.

"Yeah, perhaps a week or two earlier I had noticed a suspicious man. I told the police about it too, during their investigation into the coin. But as for details about what he looked like, I simply couldn't remember."

"Does that happen anymore?" Abigail questioned after she had written down Mr. Gruber's last reply. "Do you still see those strange visitors going into the back of the dry cleaners?"

"Since I retired and turned the place over to my son, I'm not always here at lunchtime. I go down to the diner and play checkers with some of the other old fogies. Yet to tell you the truth, I think all of Miller's friends stopped appearing right after I found that coin. From what I heard, the police were looking into Frank which made the end of those visitors seem even more suspicious."

"Mr. Gruber," asked Grant, surprising his friends, "was there anything else unusual that happened around the time you found the coin? Anything that sticks out to you?"

"Not that I can recall, son. Oh wait, well, I don't know," the old pharmacist paused for a moment and stared blankly off into the distance as if searching for a memory on the other side of the horizon. "There was one odd thing, I guess," he finally resumed. "A month or so after all this happened, I had the strangest visitor in the pharmacy. He was a country fellow, and I do mean country. He had an old, tattered felt fedora on his head and a dated thread-bare jacket. Honestly, he looked like he had just crawled in from the hills, and he spoke like it too. Reminded me of someone though, although I could never quite place who."

"What did he want?" Grant probed.

"He wanted to know about the Roman coin," replied Mr. Gruber, "asking me north of a million questions. Lots of people had been asking about it. The story had made it into the papers by that time. Yet, he wasn't asking like other people did. He seemed to be, well, investigating it, I guess. But not like you kids are. Not in the kind of way you would if you were trying to solve a mystery. He only seemed interested in trying to find out where the coin had come from. And honestly, I got the impression that he believed that there were more."

"More?" questioned Miles, unsure of what Mr. Gruber meant.

"More coins, son," the old man clarified. "More coins."

"Thank you Mr. Gruber," Abigail concluded, shutting her notebook. "We really appreciate you taking the time to share all of this with us."

"And for the sodas," added Zayne, who then with lifted eyebrows and a sly smile pointed to Abigail's bottle.

Deciphering his silent request, Abigail sighed and then nodded.

Zayne scooped up her bottle and took a large swig.

"You're welcome kids," answered Mr. Gruber, "stop in and see me again some time. Now I'd better head down to the diner. I've got some checkers waiting for me. And I bet that not even that grumpy old know-it-all Gary Knapp can guess the world-record weight for a largemouth bass."

Chapter Five

While Abigail, Miles, Grant, and Zayne interviewed Mr. Gruber, the rest of the Bible Club spent the morning down at the library. Their goal was to uncover hard evidence that the Roman coin had, in fact, been stolen.

Despite scouring the internet and scanning dozen of newspaper databases, Declan, Talia, and Tomas' efforts turned up nothing new. The best they could find were a few articles about Mr. Gruber's discovery of the coin.

Although not what they hoped for, Tomas printed each of these articles and organized them into a large blue binder, which he had begun calling the Case File.

Just past twelve thirty, Declan sat alone at a small round table in one of the library's study rooms. The tabletop before him lay bare, except for the open Case File and a strangely-shaped brown paper sack. While Tomas and Talia had each gone home to get a quick bite to eat, Declan had packed his lunch. Now he patiently waited for the Bible Club to regroup, passing the time by carefully examining the details in the various newspaper accounts.

Originally Declan had been the lone voice of opposition to the idea of starting an investigation into the coin. But after seeing both the joy and the seriousness of his friends, he was now fully devoted to seeing it through. This was classic Declan.

Cautious and thoughtful by nature, the young man never rushed into anything. Yet when he made a commitment, watch out! Declan was all in.

You could even see this approach in his faith.

As the only son of a pastor, one could easily assume that Declan followed Jesus because others expected it of him. However, nothing could be further from the truth. From an early age, he had never taken faith for granted but instead tried to understand what Christianity meant and who God wanted him to be. For this reason, Declan's relationship with Jesus had a genuine depth that went far beyond his years.

And Declan lived out what he believed too, which was precisely how the Bible Club had come about.

Friendly and kind, Declan could have been the most popular boy in school. There was only one thing holding him back. He was so friendly and so kind that he wouldn't dismiss people who weren't cool. It hadn't really been an issue until he had entered middle school. But by then, circles of people had begun to form, with rules about who you could and could not hang out with. Declan, however, refused to play by those rules and associated with anyone and everyone.

The truth be told, although this kept him from being the most popular boy in school, it secretly made Declan the most admired.

Of course, no one called Zayne cool.

Part absent-minded genius and part circus clown, the other kids had been making fun of the boy with the wild red hair for years. But Declan didn't care. The two first met at church, and they had been close friends ever since.

Tomas wasn't cool either. The child of poor immigrants, he wore second-hand clothing and didn't fit well into his mostly white middle-class school. Declan noticed and reached out.

Before his new friendship with Declan, Tomas had struggled. Afterwards, he flourished.

Miles wasn't poor, he had excellent grades, and he definitely wasn't a clown. But sadly, one thing kept him on the outside of the in-crowd—the wheelchair. Most kids simply didn't know how to interact with him, so they just didn't. One day Declan found out Miles was a Christian. They sat together at lunch ever since.

Like Declan, Abigail could have been a member of the highest circles. She was bright, talented, and outgoing. But she spent little time thinking of social status. Instead, Abigail concerned herself with faith, family, and friends.

With so much in common, it came as no surprise that Declan and Abigail had been pals as far back as they both could remember.

One Sunday at church, Declan's father had given a sermon on the importance of community. This had been the source of Declan's idea for the Bible Club. Having known Chief for years, Declan asked him if he would consider leading a Bible study for some of his friends. The retired policeman loved God and young people, and hated being bored, so he immediately agreed.

From there, Declan invited Zayne, Miles, Tomas, and Abigail. Abigail had brought her little sister Grace and her new friend Talia, who had just moved to town. Then recently, Miles invited Grant.

The club was a huge success. And it all started because one young man put his faith into action.

Certainly when it had begun, no one could have guessed that this group of kids investigating the Bible would turn into a group of kids investigating mysteries. Yet that is exactly what had occurred.

As Declan finished examining the Case File, he closed the binder and leaned back in his chair, throwing his arms back behind his head.

Just then, Tomas returned.

"Did you find anything new?" Tomas asked, dropping himself into one of the chairs at the table.

"No, not a thing."

"Didn't you eat your lunch?" inquired Tomas, pointing to the brown paper sack in the middle of the table.

"That's not my lunch," replied Declan.

Next, Talia and Abigail arrived, pulling the study room door closed behind them.

"Hi guys," Abigail said, "Talia was just telling me about the articles you found. We had a pretty interesting morning down at the pharmacy. I can't wait to tell you about it."

"We can't wait to hear about it," answered Tomas, reaching for the Case File and opening it up to the newspaper articles.

Noticing the paper sack, Talia looked at Declan. "Is that your lunch?"

Declan shook his head 'no' as Miles and Grant opened the door.

"Hey everyone," Miles began enthusiastically, "I hope your morning has been as productive as ours."

"Well," Declan said, rising to his feet and standing behind his chair, "we didn't really find much. I'd love to hear about the interview with Mr. Gruber though. Where's Zayne so we can get started?"

"He's out front eating," responded Miles, tossing his thumb over his shoulder like a hitchhiker. "We stopped to get some hot dogs from a street vendor and Zayne had only finished scarfing down his first three. He's a bottomless pit. Hey, is that your lunch?" Miles added, noticing the brown bag in the middle of the table. "I don't think you are allowed to have that in here."

"No worries," Declan answered casually, "it's not my lunch."

Finally, Zayne appeared at the doorway, having somehow managed to get ketchup from his recent hot dogs all over his forehead. On his feet, he still wore the green froggy boots.

"Hi Talia…hi Tomas…hi Declan," he exclaimed happily.

"Hi," Declan smiled as he reached for the paper bag in the center of the table. Putting his hand inside, he pulled out a tennis shoe and tossed it to Zayne.

"My Mom found that last night in the laundry hamper," said Declan.

The redhead erupted in gratitude.

"How'd you know it was his?" inquired Talia with a grin.

"Last month I found that same shoe in our doghouse."

When the laughter had died down, the friends squeezed themselves around the small table to discuss their morning adventures.

First, Talia updated Abigail, Miles, Grant, and Zayne on their findings, showing them the articles in Tomas' Case File. Everyone expressed disappointment that they hadn't found the evidence they were looking for, however those who had been to the pharmacy did their best to encourage the researchers. Next, Abigail opened her notebook. She then proceeded to recount the interview with Mr. Gruber, sparing no details. There certainly had been some revelations. Rough characters coming and going from the back of the dry cleaners. Some of these visitors having been seen only days before the coin was discovered in the gumball machine. A strange hobo hunting after more coins. The library team grew more and more excited with each disclosure.

"Well, all in all, I think we are off to a pretty good start," Tomas said as he took the Case File back from Zayne. "But where do we go from here?"

"Jolly good question," Talia echoed.

"I think we should track down the boy who found the coin," declared Abigail as she closed her notebook.

"I think so too," agreed Miles. "What was his name again?"

"Alex Townsend," Zayne replied.

Declan was unsure.

"I don't know guys," he said skeptically. "He was only a little kid, and this happened twenty years ago. Do you think he'll remember anything about it?"

"Maybe not," offered Abigail, "but I do think we need to try. There were only two people involved in the discovery of the coin, and I don't think we should overlook one of them just because they were young."

"You're right," Declan conceded, rising again from his chair and beginning to pace as best he could in the tight quarters. "A group of kid investigators shouldn't be overlooking someone because of their age. And who knows? Perhaps he will remember something that will help. Now the question is, 'how do we find him?'"

"We could search for him on the internet," Talia suggested.

"I already did," Zayne said while suddenly discovering the ketchup on his forehead, "but I didn't find anything. Does anyone have a napkin or something?"

Talia handed him a tissue.

"Let's just try the phone book," said Miles.

"What's a phone book?" Declan asked.

48

"Are you kidding?" replied Miles with wide eyes.

"No."

"The phone book is what our parents used when they wanted to find someone," Abigail explained. "It's just a huge book filled with everyone in town."

"Technically," Zayne laughed, "the book isn't filled with everyone in town, but rather the phone numbers and addresses of everyone in town. Could you imagine a book filled with everyone in town? It would be a little bit cramped in there."

Abigail gave him a nasty look.

"But what if he doesn't live here anymore," Talia interjected. "That was a long time ago."

"You may be right," responded Abigail, "but it's worth a try. I'll go see if I can get one from the reference librarian."

A few minutes later, Abigail returned with a phone book. Placing it on the table in front of Talia, Abigail watched as her friend flipped the pages to the letter T. Running her index finger down the list of names, Talia would then turn a page or two and do it again. Finally, she came across Townsend.

"Blimey," Talia declared with disgust, "there are five Townsends and none of them are named Alex. What do we do now?"

"Maybe one of them is his mom or dad," said Declan, trying to be encouraging, "or maybe a relative of some kind. What are the names?"

Talia began reading. "Ai Townsend, J. Townsend, Rebecca Townsend, Robert Townsend, and Z. Townsend."

"Z. Townsend," Abigail grinned. "I wonder if that Z stands for Zayne."

"Unlikely," answered Zayne, using his bookish know-it-all tone. "The name Zayne is not ranked in the top one hundred baby names of the past one hundred years. More likely, the Z stands for Zachary which was fifty-eighth on the list."

"I was just kidding," Abigail said, rolling her eyes. "And besides, why are you looking up baby names?"

"I needed names for my mouse and my hamster. Although, I wasn't sure if naming them would be a good idea since I'd be taking them back. But I got tired of calling them just 'mouse' and 'hamster.' I decided on Vincent for the hamster. It was the ninety-sixth most popular name and it reminded me of Vincent van Gogh. The hamster seemed artsy and unstable, like van Gogh, so I thought it might be appropriate. Anyway, I went with Alice for the mouse. I've always liked *Alice in Wonderland*, and for some reason, people often say that I remind them of the Mad Hatter. I'm not really sure why? Did you know that Alice is the sixty-seventh most popular girl's name? Oh and by the way, Abigail is ninety-ninth and Grace is eighty-second. Sorry, none of the rest of you were ranked."

"Well, five names isn't too bad," remarked Tomas, completely ignoring the bizarre conversation between Zayne and Abigail. "Let's try calling them. Then if one of them leads to Alex Townsend, we could go over for an interview. But I don't know if I can do it today. I've only got about an hour before my dad wanted me home. We're visiting my uncle tonight."

"I can't go anywhere else today either," Miles grumbled. "My brother is in something or other at church, and Mom said that I had to be there. I have to be home no later than two."

"And I've got practice at two-thirty," Grant added.

"Well," said Declan thoughtfully, "if you guys don't mind, maybe the rest of us can do it. I'd really like to try today. It might help us know if there really is something to investigate or whether or not we are at a dead end."

"That's fine with me," answered Tomas. "If you wind up going to interview him, maybe Miles, Grant, and I could stay here and keep searching through the library records. At least, until we each have to go."

Miles and Grant agreed.

So Declan, Abigail, Talia, and Zayne were placed in charge of hunting down Alex Townsend. First, Abigail carefully recorded each of the names, addresses, and phone numbers. Next, she and Talia used the phone in the library's lobby to try and call each name. While the girls worked, Declan and Zayne got a map from the reference desk. Using a copy of Abigail's list, the two boys examined the map, trying to find each location. When the calls were completed they all met back in the study room.

The phone calls hadn't been very successful.

Two numbers were no longer correct. One number was busy. And one number didn't answer. They were, however, able to eliminate one name. Z. Townsend was no relation to Alex.

During their examination of the map, Zayne and Declan had discovered that the four remaining addresses were all within a few blocks of the number two bus route. So Abigail, Talia, Declan, and Zayne decided that they would simply try visiting each one.

With the destinations marked on their map, Abigail, Declan, and Talia gathered up their things, said goodbye to the others, and headed out for the bus stop.

Of course, Zayne was going too, but he had set down the shoe that Declan had returned and he couldn't find it. But after locating it under the table, Zayne added his own hasty goodbyes and rushed after his friends.

The strange rubber squeaking sound caused the entire library to stop and look up. What they saw was quite a sight. A redheaded boy wearing frog-faced goulashes, with a single tennis shoe thrown over his shoulder, was half-bounding and half-waddling his way toward the door. For the librarian, the sound of the repetitious squeaks became simply too much, and she gave the boy a loud, "shhh."

While continuing his rapid exit, looking even more comical as he tried to soften the landing of each boot, Zayne turned his head toward the librarian and quietly said, "Sorry." Unfortunately, he turned his head at the precise moment when he should have been looking where he was going. As a result, Zayne missed the doorway and smacked directly into the wall, causing him to fall on his bottom. The entire library gasped.

"I'm okay," Zayne shouted, jumping to his feet. But realizing that he had just yelled in the library, he frowned. "I'm okay," Zayne repeated, this time in a shrill whisper that somehow managed to be louder than his previous shout. With everyone still staring at him, he gave a final awkward smile and then dashed out the door.

The librarian dropped her head down upon her desk.

Chapter Six

Just down the street from the library, the four investigators sat together on bench, waiting for the arrival of the bus.

"Okay," Abigail began, looking down at her notebook, "the addresses follow the bus loop. And they are almost in alphabetical order except that J. Townsend comes last. So we start by looking for Ai Townsend. That's an unusual name isn't it?"

"I don't think I have any room to comment," said the boy wearing the rubber boots.

"What was the first address?" Talia asked, trying to peer over Abigail's shoulder.

"24 Elm," answered Abigail without looking up, "which is a couple of blocks behind the old grocery store."

Just then, the number two could be seen coming up the street.

"Well, here we go," said Declan, rising to his feet. When the bus arrived and had begun rolling to a stop, Declan lifted his backpack off the ground, slung it over his shoulder, and approached the door. The others arose and formed a line behind him. After letting out a weary sigh, the bus completed its stop and the door swung open. A young man with long hair and freckles sat behind the wheel.

"Hey Zayne," the twenty-something driver greeted as the friends climbed aboard.

"Hi Jon," Zayne replied.

Taken aback, Zayne's friends gave him a look of surprise.

"The children's museum is on this route," the redhead explained, "and I volunteer there a couple of days a week after school. Here's my bus pass," he added, turning to the driver and holding out a blue, laminated card. "Can my friends get day passes?"

"Sure," Jon answered as he pulled three small yellow papers from beneath his seat. "They are four dollars per person."

Abigail, Declan, and Talia each gave the driver a five dollar bill. He, in turn, gave each of them a dollar and a pass.

As usual for this route, the passengers had their pick of seats. The only others aboard were a sleepy-looking teenager, sitting in the rear of the bus, and a young mother with an infant daughter, about halfway back on the left. The investigators choose the two foremost rows on the right, with the boys in front of the girls.

"Where are you going, Zayne?" the driver asked as he closed the door and pulled the bus away from the curb.

"*Stewart's Market.*"

"Sure," Jon nodded, "be there in a couple of minutes."

"Thanks."

As the bus rumbled down the street, the four investigators sat silently, each lost in their own thoughts.

And Jon was as good as his word. In less than five minutes, the Bible Club members found themselves standing on the sidewalk in front of the grocery.

After quickly walking the two blocks over to twenty-four Elm, they stood gazing at a small white cottage in significant disrepair.

Encircling the property stood a wooden fence with peeling paint. It had lost one out of every three pickets. The long, weary front porch had several missing floor boards and its roof had been

54

propped up in one corner by a two-by-four. At the crest of the house, particle board replaced an attic window and a gutter dangled menacingly forward like an accusing finger. It appeared as if a huff and a puff might blow the whole thing down.

"Well this looks inviting," Talia remarked sarcastically.

Carefully, the crew made their way to the front door.

Abigail knocked. There was a long silence. Abigail knocked again. Still no reply.

The investigators exchanged disappointed looks.

"Let me try once more," Abigail stated. Then she rapped on the door as hard as she could.

This time, the high-pitched bark of a small dog could be faintly heard. Like an approaching siren, the yapping grew louder and louder until a tiny scratching noise emanated from the other side of the door. Next came the muffled commands of a woman; followed by the clamor of a small struggle. Apparently the woman won the fight, for the sounds of the dog soon faded. Then, after a brief interlude of silence, the deadbolt suddenly unlatched and the front door opened slightly.

The face of a middle-aged Asian woman appeared in the opening.

"Yes," she said with a heavy Chinese accent.

"Hi," began Talia, "are you Ai Townsend?"

"Yes," answered the woman.

"We are looking for a young man named Alex Townsend. Are you by any chance related?"

"Yes."

A sense of excitement grew among the four friends.

"Is he here?"

"Yes."

"Would you mind if we speak with him?" Talia continued.

"Yes."

This reply caught Talia a bit off guard. "Yes, we can speak with him," she inquired politely, "or yes you mind?"

"Yes," the woman answered once more still peering at them from the crack in the door.

Talia had grown confused by the woman's answers and was unsure of what to say next. Declan came to her rescue.

"Mam," he said with a smile, "a friend of ours told us a remarkable story about a coin that Alex found when he was a little boy. We were hoping to ask him a few questions. Could we speak to Alex for just a couple of minutes?"

The woman gave the same reply. However, she made no attempt to open the door or to go and get Alex. After an awkward silence, Zayne spoke.

"Forgive my impertinence," he said kindly, "but is there any chance that you are a lumberjack?"

Completely caught off-guard, Abigail, Declan and Talia looked at Zayne in complete horror. Yet Zayne, acting as if the question were perfectly normal, waited patiently for the woman's reply.

"Yes," she answered.

The others stared in total disbelief. Zayne turned to them and whispered, "She doesn't speak English." Suddenly the entire interaction made perfect sense.

"Thank you," Talia offered, taking a step away from the door and bowing slightly. The woman smiled and returned the bow. Abigail, Declan, and Zayne followed suit. A moment later, the investigators were back on the sidewalk in front of the house.

"Are you a lumberjack?" Abigail declared, glaring at Zayne.

"I suspected that she had no idea what we were talking about," he calmly replied. "I just wanted to test my theory."

"Are you a lumberjack?" Abigail repeated. "How about next time you just ask if they speak English?"

"If I had asked her if she spoke English, she simply would have said 'yes.'"

Trapped by Zayne's logic, Abigail was at a loss for words.

"Well, the point is, that didn't get us anywhere," interjected Declan.

"I think it did," Talia replied. "We can certainly rule her out. There's no way she could be related to Alex Townsend. And elimination is progress."

"I suppose that's true," Declan nodded.

After literally marking the name off their list, the four Bible Club members walked back to the bus stop.

Following a fifteen minute wait, the number two returned, having completed one full lap of its route. The four friends climbed back aboard and took their previous seats. From there, another short ride ensued. This time to four Applewood Court, Apartment C, where they were hoping to find Rebecca Townsend.

The apartment sat on the second floor of a dilapidated low-income complex about a half mile from where the bus had dropped them off. Apparently once a motel, all of the apartment doors opened outward toward the parking lot. An uncovered metal balcony, accessible by a rusty staircase on the building's east side, circled the upper level. After scaling the stairs and finding the correct door, the investigators had mixed feelings. They hoped that they might find Alex Townsend, but for his sake, they hoped he didn't live here.

Just as before, Abigail knocked. But unlike before, they received an immediate response.

A blaring television was silenced. Followed by the exclamation of a few unsavory words. Footsteps then approached the door. Yet the door didn't open. Instead, a hand pushed apart the blinds that covered the apartment's large front window. A pair of unfriendly, green eyes peered out at them.

"What do you want?" a young woman's voice shouted from the other side of the glass.

"Sorry to bother you," Declan said nervously, "but are you Rebecca Townsend?"

"I am…so what?"

"Well, uh, you see," Declan continued, now even more nervous than before, "we are trying to locate Alex Townsend. And, well, uh, we aren't sure how to find him. So, we, uh, we wondered if, perhaps, you might know him. Or, uh, if you might be related to him."

"I don't know an Alex Townsend," the girl yelled. "Now leave me alone."

Just then, a previously unnoticed police car came to a slow stop in front of the apartment complex. And when the eyes in the window spotted the car, the blinds were instantly released.

A second later, the door to the apartment flew open and Rebecca Townsend dashed out, pushing her way past Abigail,

Declan, Talia, and Zayne. In a heartbeat, she leapt down the rusty stairway. Then once at the bottom, she raced down an ally that led behind the building.

But the police caught sight of her.

Instantly, two officers emerged from the squad car and were in pursuit.

With mouths open wide, the four friends stood speechless. After a full minute, Declan finally broke the silence.

"Did that really just happen?" he asked the others.

"Yes," Zayne responded, scratching his head, "yes it did."

As the investigators slowly made their way down to street level, Rebecca Townsend emerged from the alley, followed closely by the two officers. This time, however, she had her hands behind her back and wore a pair of handcuffs.

"I didn't help him steal those car stereos," she declared angrily. "I wasn't even there."

"How'd you know it was car stereos that were stolen?" replied the tall dark-haired officer who had been driving the car. "We never said anything about car stereos." As the men led the girl past the members of the Bible Club, the same officer took notice of Declan.

"Hey, Declan," he said with a smile, "what are you doing here?"

"Hi, Officer Sullivan," answered Declan, "we were just looking into an old mystery that Chief had been telling us about. I'm sorry if we got in your way."

"You didn't," Officer Sullivan replied as he and his colleague led Rebecca to the squad car. "Just be careful around here. This isn't exactly the best neighborhood. Hey, say hello to Chief for me."

"I will, bye."

The officers then deposited their prisoner into the backseat of the car and drove away.

"Well," began Abigail, "I suppose we can mark another name off our list."

"I suppose we can," confirmed Talia.

The four friends then began their journey back to the bus stop.

After another short wait, Jon the bus driver carried them off once again, this time in search of the third name on their list—Robert Townsend.

Now nearing four o'clock, the friends found themselves looking up at a shabby box-shaped duplex situated on a tiny hill. If the phone book was correct, the home on the left-side belonged to Robert Townsend. After navigating a set of steep concrete stairs, Abigail, Talia, Declan, and Zayne made their way to the front door. However, as they prepared to knock, they overheard voices coming from the rear of the building.

"I'll give you thirty bucks for it?" a thin, scratchy voice offered.

"Thirty bucks," a second voice replied, "this is a top of the line car stereo. You can't get one of these at the store for less than two hundred."

"Yeah, but look at how these lines were cut," the first voice said. "It looks like you ripped this out of someone's car."

"What? Come on. Jimmy you've known me for years. Would Robert Brentley Townsend try to sell you a stolen car stereo?"

"Yes, he would."

The investigators looked uncomfortably at one another.

"Blimey, that appears to be our man," Talia exclaimed. "What do we do?"

"Well," Declan shrugged, "I guess we go around back and talk to him."

"Is that a good idea?" inquired Abigail.

"No, probably not," replied Declan, having already begun walking, "but let's do it anyway."

After making their way around back, the investigators could see a tall, wiry man holding a car stereo under one arm. He was getting into a rusty pick-up truck. A second man, standing on a small patio, held a fist full of cash. The second man called out to the first as the truck pulled away.

"You got a great deal, Jimmy. Tell your friends that I've got more stereos at great prices."

Young, muscular, and unshaven, the man on the patio stood beside a stack of car stereos piled upon a lounge chair. He looked mean and dishonest, but when he noticed the investigators, he gave them his best fake smile.

"How's it going," he said in a poor attempt at friendliness. "You must have heard about my stereos for sale. I've got some great stuff here. Real cheap too. What are you interested in?"

"Actually, we aren't here for a stereo. We were just wondering if you happened to be Robert Townsend," Declan asked, already knowing the answer.

The fake smile on the man's face was quickly replaced with a look of distrust.

"Yeah, I'm Robert Townsend. Why do you kids care?"

"We don't mean to bother you," Declan continued in a soft voice, trying to show the man that they meant him no harm. "It's just that we are looking for someone named Alex Townsend and wondered if you might be related."

"We're not," came the man's curt reply. "So unless you want to buy a stereo, get out of here."

Amazingly, just as soon as Robert Townsend had finished his sentence, a familiar police car appeared, pulling in near where the pick-up had been parked.

The angry young man grabbed a nearby blanket and threw it over top of the pile of stereos.

When Officer Sullivan and his partner emerged from either side of their cruiser, they were momentarily caught off guard by the sight of the children. However they said nothing, instead focusing their attention on the task at hand.

"Hi, Robert," Officer Sullivan began, using a familiar tone, "what do you have under that blanket?"

"Hey, Sully," Robert replied in an overly casual way. "There ain't nothing important under the blanket. I was just talking to these nice kids here…about the weather…when you pulled up. Nice seeing you Sully, but I've got to get going to work now."

"Uh, not quite so fast, Robert. Your sister told us that you've been up to no good, and that we might find you selling some stolen property."

"She's a no good liar," Robert replied ferociously. "I'm not selling any hot stereos."

"How did you know I was talking about stereos?" Sullivan asked with a smile. "I didn't say stereos."

Five minutes later, Robert Townsend sat handcuffed in the back seat of the police car. But he wasn't alone. Beside him, his sister Rebecca Townsend stared angrily out the side window. She refused to look at her brother, having overheard him call her a 'no good liar.'

Before the police carried away the thieves, the young investigators explained to the officers how they had managed to show up at both places.

"So you see," said Declan, "we have been going straight down the list of Townsends from the phone book."

"Amazing," Sullivan's partner marveled. "I couldn't believe it when we got out of the car and you four were standing here."

"Me either," chuckled Sullivan. "What are the chances that we would both be looking for a pair of Townsends?"

"The odds improve given that they were brother and sister," answered Zayne, "but I'd still calculate it at about fifty thousand to one."

"Well, I'll leave the math to you," Sullivan grinned. "Let's just hope the next name on your list isn't a burglar."

The two officers took their places in the front of the squad car.

As they began to pull away, Sullivan called out to the children from his open window.

"Be careful you guys," he said. "I've never had an adventure that didn't also include some danger."

When the four friends were alone, Declan looked at the others.

"Did *that* really just happen?" he asked.

"Yes, yes it did," Zayne replied without the slightest hint of emotion.

The afternoon had passed and early evening had begun as the friends returned once more to the bus stop. Having again boarded Jon's number two, the tired investigators enjoyed a chance to rest. Talia even leaned against the window and closed her eyes. But it wasn't long before they were off the bus and back on their feet, walking through a well-maintained older neighborhood.

This time, their destination turned out to be a picturesque cape cod, quite a contrast to the three previous stops.

The home looked lovely with fresh yellow paint and green shutters. Its hedges were neatly trimmed, and the flower beds were weed-free and full of blooms.

"Now we're talking," Abigail proclaimed. "J. Townsend is probably not selling car stereos out of the back of this place."

After knocking on the front door, a short white-haired woman with tiny wire spectacles answered.

"Hello there," she greeted them warmly, "what can I do for you?"

"Hi," Abigail said, returning the woman's smile, "by any chance are you J. Townsend?"

"Yes, honey," the little old lady replied. "I'm JoAnn Townsend."

"Wonderful," Abigail continued, delighted that they had found the fourth name on their list, "we are actually looking for an Alex Townsend, and we were hoping that you might be able to help us. By any chance do you know Alex?"

"Why certainly I do. I'm Alex's Grandmother. Come inside and have a cookie."

Feeling both triumphant and relieved, the four members of the Bible Club made their way into a small parlor just off the main entryway. Despite their protests, the kind old woman insisted that they each have a glass of milk and a cookie (or two) before they talked. After briefly disappearing into the kitchen, she soon returned with four glasses of milk and a silver tray covered in homemade gingersnaps.

With a mouth half-full of cookie, Zayne asked if Alex lived with her.

"No, honey, but Alex visits nearly every day. In fact, I'm expecting Alex anytime."

"That's great!" Talia exclaimed, nearly spilling her milk amidst her excitement.

For the next several minutes, JoAnn Townsend kept the four investigators in conversation, asking them all about their school and their activities and their Bible Club. But just as Abigail began telling their new friend the reason that they were looking for Alex, the little old woman interrupted her.

"Wait, honey, just a minute," JoAnn said. "I see Alex coming up the sidewalk now."

The members of the Bible Club all turned as the front door opened.

"Hi Grams," Alex Townsend declared. "Who are your friends?"

Abigail, Declan, and Talia's mouths dropped open.

"But…but you're a girl," Abigail stammered.

"Were you expecting a boy?" replied the young woman standing in the doorway. "I get that a lot. My real name is Alexandria, but I've always preferred Alex. Guess I'm a bit of a tom boy."

When the initial shock was over and Alex had joined them in the sitting room, the children explained the mix up. Alexandria and her Grandmother both laughed heartily. Abigail, Declan, and Talia laughed too, on the outside. But on the inside, they were extremely discouraged. This, they believed, had been their last chance to find the boy who had discovered the Roman coin. Now their investigation appeared to have hit a dead end.

(Zayne, however, didn't laugh or appear discouraged. He was too busy stuffing his face with handful after handful of Grandma Townsend's gingersnaps.)

At quarter to six, the four children excused themselves from the home of their new friends.

The short walk back to the bus stop seemed much longer amidst their disappointment. All afternoon they had circled the city and they had nothing to show for it.

Following a short wait at the bus stop, the now familiar number two came rolling down the street. With long, tired faces, Abigail, Declan, Talia, and Zayne boarded the empty bus.

"You guys look sad," Jon the bus driver said as the friends took their seats. "Had a bad day?"

"Yeah, I guess you could say that," Declan said sorrowfully. "We spent hours looking for someone and didn't find him."

"Bummer," Jon replied while checking his mirrors as he merged into traffic. "Whoever you were looking for must have been pretty important."

"Well, he was to us," Abigail explained. "Twenty years ago, he found a valuable coin on the sidewalk and put it into a gumball machine."

"Oh, so you're looking for Alex Townsend," Jon said mildly.

"How did you know that?" Talia gasped.

The bus driver laughed.

"I knew that," he grinned, "because I'm Alex Townsend."

Chapter Seven

With great dexterity, the waitress returned, balancing five plates of hamburgers upon a single tray.

"Okay, you got the double burger with fries, no tomato," she said, handing a plate to Alex. "You were the turkey burger, no fries," she continued as she gave Abigail a plate.

Effortlessly, the waitress pulled two more plates off the tray with one hand.

"You both got burgers with fries," she added, offering Declan and then Talia their food.

One meal remained on the tray. The waitress couldn't suppress a smile.

"And you got the monster burger, extra tomato and pickles, mayonnaise instead of ketchup, with a double order of fries."

Zayne licked his lips while snatching his plate.

Alex's shift had ended at six o'clock, and he had invited the investigators to join him for a bite to eat. The group of five now sat at *The Hamburger Diner*, one of the most famous landmarks in town.

The sixties style diner was known far and wide for its fantastic burgers and cheap prices. No matter the time of day you always had trouble finding a seat. Luckily, they had caught a short lull in the dinner rush. A small booth sat vacant. Abigail and Talia had squeezed in on one side. Declan and Zayne had squeezed in on the other. Alex had taken the end, having pulled over an unused chair from a nearby table.

"So, you really found another Alex Townsend?" the bus driver laughed as he picked up his hamburger. "You must have been totally caught off guard when a girl walked in."

"I wasn't," Zayne said between two long slurps of his orange soda.

Abigail, Declan, and Talia looked at him in disbelief.

"What are you talking about?" Abigail snipped. "You were just as surprised as the rest of us."

"No I wasn't," Zayne explained calmly, preparing to cram five French fries into his mouth at once. "I noticed an engraved picture frame sitting on the fireplace mantel. It was a picture of Grandma Townsend and a young woman. The inscription read, 'To the best Grams in the whole world. I love you so much, Alexandria.' When I saw the frame, I reasoned that we had the wrong Alex."

As soon as he had finished speaking, the five fries disappeared.

Abigail stared at him in disbelief.

"Then why didn't you say something?" she demanded.

"The gingersnaps were so good, I didn't want to leave," Zayne mumbled in reply as he shoved three more fries into an already full mouth.

While rubbing her temples, Abigail took a deep breathe, apparently trying to control her temper.

Sensing the need to quickly change the subject, Declan turned to Alex and asked him why he now went by the name of Jon.

"Well," Alex answered after he finished swallowing another bite of hamburger, "Jonathan is actually my middle name, but it was my dad's first name. He died when I was fourteen, and I decided to start going by Jon. It was kind of a tribute to him, I guess. But a lot of people still call me Alex, and I answer to that too."

"I'm so sorry about your Dad," Talia offered softly. "What happened?"

"He'd been really, really sick for most of my life with a rare genetic disorder. There were some good times, but it was usually pretty tough, especially on my mom. But let's not talk about the sad stuff. Why are you guys interested in that old coin? And what is it that you wanted to ask me?"

"A friend of ours told us the story," Declan replied as he pulled a napkin from a dispenser in the middle of the table, "and we just thought the whole thing seemed strange and interesting."

"Especially the part about the coin simply laying in the middle of the sidewalk," Abigail interjected.

"Right," Declan agreed while wiping some stray mustard off his fingers.

"So we know it's a long shot," he continued, "but we wondered if we might be able to find an explanation. Obviously it happened twenty years ago so we understand if you don't remember."

"Well, I was a little kid," Alex explained, "but I actually do remember it. At least, I think I do. Have you ever had an experience that people talked about over and over again, and you've heard the story so many times that you aren't quite sure if your memory is of the actual events or just the story people keep telling?"

"I know what you're talking about," said Zayne while licking the residue of French fry salt off his already empty plate.

"When I was about five," he resumed, now waving the plate around as he talked, "we once went to the science museum and signed up to do a lab. Apparently we were supposed to build a bridge out of marshmallows and toothpicks. But while the lab assistant was giving us the instructions, I secretly ate all of our marshmallows. Can you believe I'd do something like that? Talia, are you going to eat your pickle? Thanks." With his free hand, Zayne grabbed the pickle and gobbled it down. Then he continued. "So anytime we have company over, someone in my family retells that story. Now it's kind of like you said, Jon…I mean Alex. I'm not sure if I actually remember doing it or whether I'm just remembering what everyone says that I did."

Zayne set down his plate and took a final slurp of his soda.

"Although come to think of it," he added, "I do have a vague memory of walking around the museum with this really stale taste in my mouth."

As often happened whenever Zayne finished a story, everyone was speechless.

Following a moment to refocus his thoughts, Declan then asked Alex if he would be willing to share, as best he could, what happened the day that he found the coin.

"Sure," Alex replied.

The young bus driver sat back in his chair and crossed his legs. Abigail pulled out her pink pen and notebook and prepared to take notes.

"So I kind of remember being in the drug store," Alex began, "and my mom being upset about something. I'm not sure exactly what upset her, but it usually had to do with money. With my Dad being sick, he couldn't work, and my mom needed to take care of him most of the time. She had some part time jobs here and there, but we mostly got by on a little bit of cash that my grandparents could give us. Anyway, my mom sent me outside because I was being rowdy, which I don't really remember, but that's what she always says when she tells the story. Well, apparently, I had to wait for her for a long, long time. It was boring, so I started playing some kind of game, running up and down the sidewalks. That's when I found the coin."

"Do you actually recall finding the coin?" Abigail asked.

"Yeah, I do. I have this image in my mind of this enormous shiny gold object laying on the sidewalk. It's funny though. Years later, I saw the coin again. It really wasn't very big at all, only about the size of a nickel. I guess to a five-year-old it just seemed huge. You know, I can still picture the face on the coin. It was a handsome face, but it had this big sloping nose that came out to a sharp point. And the man's hair was full of leaves. I know now that it was a Roman Emperor, but back then I remember thinking it must be George Washington."

"How did you see the coin again?" Talia wondered.

"Several months after I found it, the police actually gave us the coin. No one had claimed it, and so it came back to me. Although that wasn't when I got a look at it. For years, my mom kept the coin in a safety deposit box down at the bank. She always called it my college fund. When I graduated high school we were planning to sell it and use the money to pay for me to go to college. Actually, several times, someone asked to buy the coin, but Mom always said 'no.' It was my college fund, and no matter how bad things got, she was determined to save it for my education. Eventually though, things changed. Dad just kept getting worse and money just kept getting tighter. Then after my twelfth birthday, mom had to put it up for auction. That was when I saw the coin again. We got almost fifteen thousand dollars for it, and you'd think that would have made my mom happy, but it didn't. She cried all that night. I think she knew the coin was the only possible way we'd ever be able to afford for me to go to college. And, she was right."

"You didn't get to go to college?" Abigail wondered.

"No. At least, not yet," answered Alex with a half-smile. "I'm trying to save up enough money doing this." He pointed to his bus driver's uniform. "It's going to take a long time, yet I'm not going to give up. I want to be an architect, and I can do all of my first two years at the community college. Hopefully, I can start there next fall. After that, I can transfer into the architecture program at the state school."

The entire time Alex was sharing his story, Zayne chomped on ice cubes from his glass. His loud crunching had been very distracting, and several times Abigail had given him a sharp look, trying to get him to stop. However, the red-headed boy was oblivious. And the very moment Alex finished speaking, Zayne nodded thoughtfully a couple of times, said *hmm*, and then abruptly asked if anyone else wanted dessert.

Abigail appeared to be looking for something to throw, but Alex saved him, saying that he thought some ice cream sounded great.

So Zayne called the waitress back over, and he, Alex, and Talia placed orders.

Small talk about saving for college and Alex's bus driving job carried the conversation until the waitress returned with three bowls.

"Here's your scoop of rainbow sherbet," the waitress said to Talia as she handed her the first bowl. "Here's your two scoops of double chocolate," she continued, offering the second bowl to Alex. And once again, the waitress couldn't help but smile when she got to Zayne.

"And here is your scoop of cookie dough, scoop of black raspberry, scoop of peppermint stick, and scoop of lemon."

The waitress chuckled to herself as she returned to the front counter.

While Alex, Talia, and Zayne began working on their ice cream, Abigail turned the conversation back to the discovery of the coin.

"I know it was such a long time ago," she began, "but do you happen to remember anyone else being around while you waited for your mom?"

"Well, sort of," Alex replied, preparing to drop his spoon into his bowl for a second bite. "I wouldn't say that I actually remember this, but my mom said that I told the police that there had been a girl on the sidewalk. She was older than me, and she was...well, I told them that she was dancing."

"Dancing?" questioned Talia, a bit confused.

"Yeah. I know it sounds odd, but apparently that's what I saw. Or at least, what I thought I saw."

"Can you recall what she looked like?" Declan asked, deeply intrigued by this revelation.

"Not at all. Like I said, I really don't even remember seeing her. It was just something my mom told me."

Declan nodded his understanding. He then followed up by asking Alex if he knew where he found the coin.

"I know I found it in front of the dry cleaners, but I don't have any real recollection of that either. Again, it's just part of the legend."

"Then you probably don't remember seeing anything, uh, suspicious happening at the dry cleaners?" asked Talia as she pushed her sherbet aside, half unfinished.

Alex gave her a knowing glance.

"I think I understand what's behind that question," he said. "As I've gotten older, I've heard the suspicions about Frank Miller;

how he might have been selling stolen coins. But if that's true, I didn't see anything."

There was visible disappointment on Talia's face after Alex's answer. Although very unlikely, she couldn't help but to hope for some bit of new evidence that might lead them to a criminal.

"However," their new friend added after a long pause. "I did have a strange interaction with Mr. Miller, years after finding the coin."

The eyes of the investigators suddenly grew wide with interest.

"It happened when I was about eleven or maybe twelve," Alex said, putting down his spoon and growing more serious.

"One day, my mom and I were at the pharmacy waiting in a line to pick up medicine for my dad," he continued. "To save some time, she asked me to go pick up a dress that had needed dry cleaning. So I went down to *Miller's*. At first, he acted friendly enough. But after I handed him the ticket for the dress, things changed." Alex shifted uncomfortably in his chair as if his position matched the memory. "You see, the ticket had our last name on it. And after reading the name, he gave me a nasty look. 'Oh, you're the little thief,' he said to me. Then he went and got the dress. You won't believe what happened next?"

"What?" Abigail wondered, looking up from her notebook.

"He threw the dress on the floor in front of my feet and gave me this icy stare. Needless to say, I grabbed the dress and took off."

"Beastly. What in the world did he mean?" wondered Talia.

"I have absolutely no idea. I'd never even been in there before. And after I told my mom about it, she started using a different shop. So I haven't been in there since. But that sure was weird, don't you think?"

"That's an understatement," replied Declan thoughtfully.

Meanwhile, Zayne had just finished his last bite of ice cream, but he didn't look so good. In fact, his face had turned the same shade of green as his froggy boots.

"Are you okay, Zayne?" Talia inquired, genuinely concerned.

"I don't feel so good," he answered while wrapping both of his arms around his midsection. "My stomach hurts."

"I wonder why," said Abigail sarcastically.

"We'd better get going home," Declan added, looking from Zayne to Alex, "but do you mind just one more question?"

Alex said that he didn't.

"Earlier, you told us that your family had offers for the coin before putting it up for auction. Is there anything you might be able to tell us about the people who made those offers?"

"Well, it is true that there were several offers," Alex began, "but it wasn't people. It was only one person. And yes, he was very memorable."

"Why?" Talia asked.

"Uh, well, I really don't mean this as an insult, but it's just the only way to describe him. To put it simply, he was a hillbilly."

"With an old, threadbare coat and a fedora hat." Zayne interjected, suddenly looking considerably less green.

"Yeah," Alex answered, rather surprised, "how did you know that? And do you want to hear something even stranger? Every time this guy showed up at the house, he would offer us thousands of dollars for the coin. Then he would pull a roll of hundred dollar bills right out of his pocket. Heck, the guy didn't even look like he could afford a meal, but he'd carry this huge wad of cash around with him. Crazy, right?"

"How many times did he come to your house?" inquired Talia, literally sitting on the edge of her seat.

"All together, he came about four or five times. But it was over the course of several years. He'd come and offer us money, and Mom would turn him down. About six months later, he'd show up again, offering a little bit more, and Mom would turn him down again."

"But eventually he just gave up?" Declan wondered, rubbing his chin thoughtfully.

"Exactly," Alex replied as he shrugged his shoulders. "I guess he just realized we weren't going to let him have it."

Abigail paused her frantic note taking and asked, "You don't happen to remember his name do you?"

"Oh yeah," Alex answered, pointing at Abigail excitedly. "I'm so glad you asked that. Get this. He'd have a different name every time. I'm not joking. One visit he called himself one thing, and the next visit he called himself something else. And the names weren't even close."

"Wow," Declan exclaimed. "Why'd he do it?"

"I have no idea."

"Do you remember any of the names?" Declan followed up.

"No, I'm afraid I don't. But it really was amazing. You'd think that if you were going to use a fake name you'd at least write it down so you wouldn't forget."

While he spoke, Alex gathered up all of the meal checks.

"My treat," he then added with a smile.

"We should be treating you," Declan remarked.

"No, it was my pleasure. It isn't every day that people want to listen to my old story about that coin. Hey, Zayne, you look like you're starting to feel better?"

"I am. Thanks," Zayne answered while everyone else rose from the table. "But wait. Talia, before we go…"

"What Zayne?" Talia shrugged.

"Are you going to eat the rest of that sherbet?"

Chapter Eight

Chief sat in his favorite chair, Bible open upon his lap, sipping on a large cup of steaming, hot coffee.

For more than two decades this had been a common occurrence at Chief's house.

Each and every morning it was always the same. He sat in the same chair, with the same Bible, drinking from the same coffee cup.

Day after day. Month after month. Year after year.

That time each morning had long been his favorite part of the day. And although it was a commitment, it wasn't an obligation.

The way Chief put it, beginning his day with God was like a car refueling. Life took energy and left his tank drained. Yet his quiet time replenished his tank, filling him with the greatest fuel of all—God's love.

However, Chief's Bible reading didn't only occur in the morning. And now as he studied, the clock on the wall said four-thirty. On this day, he had returned to his familiar chair in order to review a passage of Scripture that he would soon be sharing with the Bible Club.

It had been a week since their last study, and although Chief didn't know it, a lot had happened in that time. Soon his young friends would be arriving, providing him with an update regarding their investigation into the valuable Roman coin. But to be honest, Chief had barely reflected on the decades-old mystery. And although Declan had mentioned it after church, the retired policeman had no idea just how seriously the group had taken the matter.

Instead, Chief's thoughts were on God and His work, which at present meant the spiritual growth of eight amazing children.

But it hadn't always been this way.

Born Stanley Archibald Oliver, he grew up with the all-consuming dream of becoming a policeman like his father and his grandfather. The dream became a reality when, at age twenty, he was initiated into the police force. For the next two decades, he gave everything he had to his job, and people noticed. Well respected in the community and highly-regarded among his fellow officers, Stan Oliver became the youngest police chief in the city's history. It was quite an accomplishment. And although he felt proud of his achievement, he also felt something else—emptiness.

While climbing the ranks, Chief's job had been his life. He never married. He didn't have close friendships. And he neglected God.

Jesus said, "What good is it for someone to gain the whole world, yet forfeit their soul?" Despite being one of the most important and powerful people in the city, Chief had discovered the answer to Jesus' question.

It wasn't that Chief didn't believe in God. He did, but that is where it began and where it ended. However, God designed us for a relationship with Him. And this, like many other things, had been something that Stan Oliver simply hadn't made time for.

Yet all of that changed.

Chief had known Bill Gruber for years. One day, following a shoplifting case down at Gruber's pharmacy, Bill had unexpectedly invited Chief to go fishing. The policeman agreed. As the two men developed a friendship, Bill began asking Chief about his views on God. Somewhat contrary to his nature, the Christian pharmacist just listened as Chief expressed his doubts that Jesus could actually be the Son of God. Soon however, Bill had invited Chief to his men's Bible study. After declining several times, Chief eventually accepted. Over the course of the next twenty-five years, the policeman only missed the men's group twice: once for his recent knee surgery and once after being grazed in the arm by a bank robber's bullet.

Even Chief couldn't say exactly when he started following Jesus. For him, it was a process. However, on the second anniversary of his becoming police chief, Stan Oliver got baptized in the lake where he and Bill Gruber had first gone fishing. Now, the heart of the old policeman sitting in the recliner bore no resemblance to that of the young policeman of years before. The selfishness and pride of his past had been replaced with a deep gentleness and humility.

And so after he had finished preparing for the study, Chief remained in his favorite chair, nursed his coffee, and prayed for each individual member of the Bible Club. He was still there when Miles and Grant knocked at the front door. The two friends had arrived quite early. Grant wanted to discuss something with Chief, and he had asked Miles to come along.

The three talked for over thirty minutes before the other members of the Bible Club began to appear.

As usual, commotion filled the room in anticipation of the study. However, tonight there was an added excitement for the friends couldn't wait to tell Chief about their investigation into the Roman coin. Yet the study came first, as they all understood. So one by one, they took their familiar places in the living room.

"Oh wait, I almost forgot," Abigail exclaimed while everyone settled in. "Zayne, my neighbor three doors down found your missing bicycle."

"Awesome," Zayne said excitedly, "where was it?"

"In the back of his garage," answered Abigail.

"Oh, of course," Zayne declared, nodding his head up and down.

"Zayne," Abigail added cautiously like someone stepping onto ice, "I know I'm going to regret asking this, but why was your bike in my neighbor's garage?"

The redhead beamed.

"Well," he began with a knowing look, "whenever I ride over to your house, there is this little boy on a scooter who watches me the entire time."

"Yeah, that's Michael," offered Abigail. "He lives across the street, and he's always out on that scooter. But what does that have to do with it?"

"About a month ago," continued Zayne, assuming his scientific tone, "I had an excellent idea for a social experiment. It works like this. Every time I come over to your place, I park my bike at a different house. Then I sneak over to visit you." Although he was seated, Zayne demonstrated his sneaking before he continued. "My goal is to determine how long it will take before the boy asks me what's going on. So far, I've parked at ten different houses." He held up all of his fingers for clarity. "You should see his face every time I ride past. I can literally watch his brain spinning as he tries to figure out who I am and what I could possibly be doing." Zayne began to chuckle. "My guess," he finally added, "is that he thinks I'm some kind of salesman, or maybe a spy. But he still hasn't asked."

"You park your bike in the garages of perfect strangers," cried Declan.

"Sometimes. It makes the experiment more believable. But most of the time I just park on their front porch."

"Their front porch!" Declan exclaimed. "You park your bike on their front porch?"

"Of course, that is very strange," Abigail remarked casually. "However, it doesn't explain why you left the bike. Did you just forget where you parked it?"

"Not at first," answered Zayne, wagging his index finger. "You see, when I left your house, the little boy was at the end of your neighbor's driveway. Apparently, he had been watching for me to come out. Try as I might, I couldn't think of any way to sneak back over and get my bike without him realizing that I had never really gone inside your neighbor's house. So I walked home. I guess I forgot about the whole thing sometime between seven o' clock that evening and eight o' clock the next morning."

Suddenly, Grace let out a loud gasp.

"Oh my goodness," she bellowed. "That explains it."

"Explains what?" asked Tomas as he turned toward Grace.

"Every night for the past week, Michael has been standing at the end of the Carroll's driveway, just staring into their garage," Grace said as she pressed her hands against the side of her head. "He's still waiting to see if you are going to come out!"

When the resulting laughter slowly died down, Chief began to speak.

"Well," he began with his typical warm smile, "from what I've been hearing, you all have quite a bit to tell me about that old Roman coin. I'm impressed that you started an investigation, and I can't wait to hear about it. As soon as we finish our study, we'll dive right into your mystery."

Chief offered another smile and then rubbed his hands together like an eager child on Christmas morning.

"Okay," he added happily, "who wants to start us off with a prayer?"

"I will," answered Tomas.

After folding his hands upon his lap and closing his eyes, Tomas began to pray.

"Dear God, thank you for our Bible Club where we get to learn about you. And thank you for giving us such a great leader in Chief. I also pray that tonight's study would go well. Oh yeah, and help us figure out what really happened with that Roman coin. In Jesus' name, Amen."

"Thanks Tomas. Now everyone, open your Bibles to Matthew 22:23," Chief instructed while also doing so himself. "We are going to continue to look at just how special Jesus is. If you remember last time, the Pharisees had been trying to trap Jesus with an unfair question about paying a temple tax that the people didn't want to pay. But Jesus somehow managed to avoid their trap with the famous line, 'give to Caesar what is Caesars and to God what is God's.' So, who wants to pick up the story beginning in verse 23?"

"I do," said Grace before anyone else had a chance to speak.

She found the verse in her Bible and began reading.

"That same day, the Sad…Saddiest…Sad dukes…Sad ducks. Never mind. I don't want to read after all."

"That's okay, Grace," Chief comforted. "That's a hard word. It says Sadducees. Does anyone remember who the Sadducees were?"

"Yeah, I remember," Miles answered confidently. "The Sadducees were another group of Jewish leaders, but they were way different than the Pharisees. For starters, they were rich. And if I remember right, they didn't believe in life after death."

"Spot on," Talia proclaimed, "that's what verse 23 means when it says, 'the Sadducees, who say there is no resurrection, came to him with a question.'"

"Please try again, Grace," Chief encouraged, "beginning in verse 24."

"Okay," Grace replied a bit sulkily.

"'Teacher,' they said, 'Moses told us that if a man dies without having children, his brother must marry the widow and raise up offspring for us. Now there were seven brothers among us. The first one married and died, and since he had no children, he left his wife to his brother. The same thing happened to the second and third brother, right on down to the seventh. Finally, the woman died. Now then, at the resurrection, whose wife will she be of the seven, since all of them were married to her?'"

Grace looked up.

"That's really weird," she said with no hint of her former poutiness. "What are the Saddies talking about?"

"Sadducees, Grace," her sister Abigail corrected, "not Saddies."

"That's a good question," Chief acknowledged. "Does anyone understand why the Sadducees are asking Jesus this?"

"It's not a real situation, right?" Tomas inquired of Chief as he sat cross-legged on the floor beside the policeman's chair. "Didn't they just make it up?"

Chief didn't reply, but instead waited for someone else to answer Tomas' question.

"I think so," answered Talia, "but why?"

"It's another trap," said Declan passionately. "Remember, they don't believe in the resurrection, but Jesus does. This question is trying to make Jesus, and his beliefs, look stupid."

"Well, if it's another trap," Miles wondered, "how does Jesus get out of it?"

"Let's find out," Chief replied. "Keep reading, Grace."

Grace resumed.

"Jesus replied, 'You are in error because you do not know the scriptures or the power of God.'"

"Jesus is slamming them there, isn't he?" Grant interrupted unexpectedly.

"Yes," said Chief as he slowly adjusted his recliner, always mindful of his healing knee. "Does anyone know why?"

No one answered.

"He's saying that they don't know their Bibles and that they don't know how big God is," Chief explained. "To say this to a group of Jewish leaders is an incredible insult."

Chief indicated to Grace to read on.

"At the resurrection people will neither marry nor be given in marriage; they will be like the angels in heaven. But about the resurrection of the dead—have you not read what God said to you, 'I am the God of Abraham, the God of Isaac, and the God of Jacob?' He is not the God of the dead but of the living."

"Wow," exclaimed Abigail, "he blows up their story by saying that they have no idea what they're talking about."

"And the way Jesus talks about the resurrection is amazing," Tomas added, waving his arms demonstratively. "Saying that they will be like the angels, it's like he has personal knowledge about it that no one else does."

"That's because he does," grinned Miles.

"I love how he says 'I am the God of Abraham, the God of Isaac, and the God of Jacob,'" offered Talia.

"I love that too," agreed Zayne, slapping the page of his Bible affectionately. "Abraham, Isaac, and Jacob were the Fathers of the Jewish people. They are supposed to be dead. But Jesus' quote has God speaking about them in the present tense. They are supposed to be dead, but to God they aren't dead. That's life after death, and that smashes the Sadducees' beliefs. Absolutely epic!"

"Then, see how the passage ends," Declan noted, never lifting his eyes from his Bible. "When the crowds heard this, they were astonished at his teaching."

"Cool," Grant said quietly.

Having wrapped up their study, the Bible Club spent the next several minutes praying.

Their normal procedure was to have Chief start and finish the prayer time, allowing any of the children to join in between. This evening went like that too, with Declan, Abigail, Grace, and Talia each adding a prayer. However unlike most nights, after the concluding 'Amen' the kids didn't dash off to the snack table or scatter throughout the house to play games. On this night, everyone remained firmly in their seats, anxious to share with Chief everything that they had learned so far in their investigation.

Seeing their excitement, Chief kicked off the conversation.

"Alright," he said with a huge grin, settling back into his recliner, "what have you learned about our ten-thousand dollar gumball?"

The young detectives looked excitedly around the circle as they waited for someone to begin.

It was Abigail who spoke up first.

"Well, we've organized everything into our Case File," she began. "Tomas do you mind if I have it for a moment?"

Tomas had placed the large binder on the floor beside him during the study. He picked it up and passed it around the circle to Abigail.

"Of course, we haven't solved anything," Abigail said, opening the binder, "but I think we've found out some interesting facts that the police may not have known."

"Like what?" Chief asked.

"Well for starters," Abigail began, turning to a page with a copy of her notes from their interview with Bill Gruber, "about a month after discovering the coin, Mr. Gruber was visited by a mysterious stranger. This man, dressed in tattered country clothing, asked him all kinds of questions about the coin."

"And," Myles interrupted excitedly, "Mr. Gruber thought that the man's motive was to find out if there were more coins."

"And," Declan jumped in, "Alex Townsend described being visited by the same mysterious stranger. The man tried to buy the coin from his mom."

"Wait. Not exactly," corrected Zayne, throwing up both his hands. "We know that the descriptions of the two men were nearly identical, but we don't know for sure that it was the same person. We must be careful with our logic."

"You're right, Zayne," Declan acknowledged. "But, it does *seem* as if the two were visited by the same man."

Zayne nodded his approval.

His interest peaked, Chief leaned forward as best as his healing knee would allow.

"What exactly did this man look like?" he asked.

Abigail searched the page in the Case File for a direct quote.

After finding it, she said, "according to Mr. Gruber, 'He was a country fellow, and I do mean country. He had an old, tattered felt fedora on his head and a tired thread-bare jacket. Honestly, he looked like he had just crawled in from the hills, and he spoke like it too.'"

After turning a few pages in the binder, Abigail continued.

"Alex Townsend called the visitor a 'hillbilly.' Then Zayne asked him if he had a threadbare coat and fedora hat, which Alex said that he did."

"The two descriptions were spot on," Talia proclaimed. "It sure sounds like the same person."

"Wait," said Tomas eagerly, "tell Chief what you told us…about the wads of cash."

Searching through the interview notes, Abigail soon found what she was looking for.

"Every time this guy showed up at the house," she read, "he would offer us thousands of dollars for the coin. Then he would pull a roll of hundred dollar bills right out of his pocket. Heck, the guy didn't even look like he could afford a meal, but he'd carry this huge wad of cash around with him."

"And," Tomas added, nearly falling over in his excitement, "you told us that every time this stranger visited Alex he used a different last name."

"Is that true?" asked Chief seriously.

Abigail indicated that it was indeed true.

"That's not all," Miles exclaimed. "Tell him about the time Alex went into the dry cleaners."

Abigail began to talk but Declan spoke over her.

"Once, Alex's mom sent him into the dry cleaners to pick up her dress…" Declan started.

"When he was about eleven or twelve," Abigail interjected.

"Right, when he was about eleven or twelve," Declan continued. "And Mr. Miller called him a crook."

Looking down at the Case File, Abigail said, "His exact words were 'Oh, you're the little thief.'"

"Yeah," confirmed Declan, "and then he threw the dress on the floor at Alex's feet. Alex said that he had never even been in the store before, and that he had absolutely no idea what Mr. Miller could have been talking about."

Grace, who was trying very hard to understand the rapid fire conversation, asked, "Why would Mr. Miller do that?"

"The most logical explanation," Zayne replied, "is that Mr. Miller was referring to the lost Roman coin. It appears that he was accusing Alex of having stolen it. Which means…."

"Which means," Grant chimed in unexpectedly, "that the coin must have been Miller's."

"Right," confirmed Zayne, giving Grant a thumb's up. "So what was Mr. Miller doing with a rare Roman coin? And if it was his, why didn't he claim it?"

"Because it was nicked," said Talia. "I'm sorry. I mean stolen."

"Right again," Zayne congratulated with a look of satisfaction upon his face.

Chief had remained silent, carefully listening to everything his young friends had to tell him. Now that they had finished, he stood up. Then, he pressed his hands deeply into his pockets, and with a noticeable limp, circled slowly around to the back of his chair.

Several minutes passed as the others waited anxiously for Chief to speak, but he remained lost in thought. Finally, it was Grace who broke the silence.

"What happens next?" she asked.

Chief glanced first at her and then around the room at each of the children. There was a light dancing in his eyes that the members of the Bible Club had never seen before.

"Well," he answered firmly, "two things."

Before continuing, he hobbled back around to the front of his recliner and sat down.

"First, you need to keep searching for evidence that the coin was stolen. Look through every newspaper article you can find, but widen the range. Maybe it wasn't stolen from around here. Or, maybe it hadn't been stolen recently. Sometimes this stuff can be hidden for years before resurfacing."

Chief began speaking more quietly as if talking to himself.

"I know we considered those possibilities, yet maybe we still missed it."

"We'll see what we can find," declared Miles passionately.

"You said two things happen next," Abigail reminded him, "what's the second?"

Chief stared directly at her.

"I think it's time you pay a visit to Jess Evers."

Chapter Nine

After Grant pressed the doorbell, the theme song to *The Hollywood Hayseeds* could be heard reverberating behind the elegant oak doors.

He and his friends had arrived at the beautiful mansion of Jess Evers, and they waited patiently for the town's most famous resident to answer the door.

An actor of considerable success, Evers got his start by playing bit parts in movies for a major Hollywood studio. However, that was just the beginning. His natural comedic and dancing talent, combined with his easy screen presence, soon landed him a significant contract with a rival studio. Over the course of time, his movie roles continued to grow, and he became a well-regarded supporting man. But despite doing well on the big screen, Evers found his greatest success when he continued his career on television.

His versatility as an actor landed him several key roles on hit shows. But his first lead role came later in life, on the comedy *The Hollywood Hayseeds*. Jess played the father of a rural family who suddenly found themselves living in Hollywood. He won numerous awards for the show, and it was a ratings hit. Several other popular television roles followed later, but none that quite matched the success of *The Hollywood Hayseeds*. Yet as his acting career began to wind down, Evers retired to the small community where he had been born. Occasionally, he could be seen about town, fishing or boating or eating out. But, for the most part, Evers lived out a quiet retirement on his large estate.

Although the two men didn't know each other well, Chief had met Evers at a few local charity functions. So, it was Chief who arranged for the Bible Club to speak with the famous actor. Everyone agreed, however, that it would be best not to send more than four people to the interview. But since everyone wanted to meet Evers and to see his mansion, the children were once again forced to play rock-paper-scissors in order to decide who would get to go.

Tomas, Grant, Miles, and Zayne had won.

As the doorbell continued to play the familiar tune inside the mansion, Tomas and Zayne continued what had become a familiar argument.

"I still say it's cheating," Tomas fumed.

"It isn't," answered Zayne. "Watching the persons hand when you play rock-paper-scissors isn't cheating."

"But you know what they are going to do!"

"You don't know for sure. But I will admit that it does give you an advantage. For instance, if their entire fist is clenched tight then they are probably going to do rock. If all their fingers are loose then they are probably going to do paper. However, if only their top two fingers are loose then scissors."

"It sounds like cheating to me," replied an irate Tomas.

"Me too," added Miles.

As one of the huge doors began to swing open, Zayne, who wanted to get in the last word, quickly muttered, "It isn't cheating. It's just being smart."

Tomas gave him a nasty look as the large distinguished man, wearing a penguin-tailed tuxedo, stood before them. He was obviously not Jess Evers.

"Can I help you?" asked the man, who they correctly assumed was the butler.

"Yes," Miles began, trying to hide his nerves, "we are the Bible Club...well...I mean...we are part of the Bible Club. Yes, well, anyway, our friend Chief made us an appointment to interview Mr. Evers. And, well, we are here…which obviously you can see…and we hoped Mr. Evers is here…of course…so that we might talk to him…like we were under the impression that we were allowed to do…if that is still okay…which we hope it is…but if it isn't we understand."

"He is expecting you. Please come with me."

Upon entering the mansion, the four young detectives found themselves in a beautiful entryway with a long winding staircase at the back. As they followed the butler across the marble floor, every step Zayne took emitted a strange squeaking noise.

"Why are you wearing those frog boots again?" Tomas whispered to Zayne, still angry over their rock-paper-scissors argument. "I thought Declan found your other tennis shoe?"

"He did, but I lost it again. Although I don't mind, my froggy boots are really comfortable."

"You don't wear froggy boots to a millionaire's house," Miles rebuked.

"Why not?" asked Zayne.

"Isn't it obvious?" countered Miles.

"Not to me," Zayne answered sincerely.

On the far side of the room, the butler led them through a doorway which had been hidden by the winding staircase. Once inside, they found themselves staring at four enormous walls entirely covered with books.

"Mr. Evers will meet you here in a few moments," the butler told them, just before exiting through the same door which they had just entered.

As they waited, Miles, who loved to read, rolled his way over to the nearest bookshelf. He let out a high-pitched whistle as he examined the book titles.

"Wow," he exclaimed, "Tolstoy...Dostoyevsky...Solzhenitsyn. These are some of the greatest Russian writers of all times. And they look like first editions."

"What are first editions?" asked Grant, who had walked over to join Miles.

"First editions are the very original printing of a book. Look, *War and Peace*. If that's a first edition it must be worth tens of thousands."

"And over here," declared Zayne as he perused a shelf on the other side of the room. "This one is Charles Dicken's *A Tale of Two Cities*. My Dad would sure love to find this under the tree on Christmas morning. I wonder how much it's worth."

"About twenty-five thousand dollars," came an unexpected reply.

The friends turned quickly to look at the distinguished white-haired man who had entered the room undetected.

"Hi," said Miles, instantly recognizing the famous actor, "we were just looking around. What an amazing collection of books you have, Mr. Evers."

"Thank you," he replied kindly as he went and sat down in an oversized-reading chair in the center of the room. He then motioned for the children to come and join him.

Zayne came over and threw himself into a matching chair that faced Mr. Evers. And Miles rolled his wheelchair beside Zayne. Finally, after the butler returned and placed two wicker folding chairs on Zayne's far side, Tomas and Grant also took a seat.

Nearly eighty-years-old, Mr. Evers was a tall thin man with large blue eyes and a wide mouth. He was dressed casually in a pair of Khaki pants, a polo shirt, and loafers. With an upright posture, legs crossed at the knee, and his arms laying upon the chair's armrests, he looked like a king in his castle.

After asking the children their names and a few other courtesy questions, the famous actor got to the heart of the matter.

"So, if I understand correctly, you have some interest in my tribute penny."

With a somewhat confused look, Miles replied, "Well, sir, we wanted to ask you about the Roman coin that you bought at auction some time back. The coin found on the sidewalk and put into the gumball machine by Alex Townsend. Uh, we aren't familiar with your tribute penny."

"Oh yes you are," Mr. Evers answered with a subtle grin. "For they are one and the same."

Standing up and walking over to a bookshelf, the old man removed a leather bound book and then returned to his seat. After flipping the pages, he began to read, "But Jesus perceived their wickedness, and said, 'Why tempt ye me, ye hypocrites? Shew me the tribute money.' And they brought unto him a penny. And he saith unto them, 'Whose is this image and superscription?' They say unto him Caesar's. Then saith he unto them, 'Render therefore unto Caesar the things which are Caesar's; and unto God the things that are God's.'"

"That's exactly what got us started on our investigation," Tomas proclaimed.

Closing the Bible upon his lap, Mr. Evers continued, "Although it may have been a version minted in silver, a coin just like the one you are inquiring about was brought to Jesus in this familiar passage. They were quizzing him on whether or not the Jews should give the required monies, called a tribute, to the Romans. Thus, the coin obtained the nickname, tribute penny. It is significantly more collectable because of this story. Actually, ever since I started collecting, I wanted to obtain one precisely for this reason. I've always found Jesus' answer to be quite brilliant. And to own a coin like the one he was talking about, well, it is the kind of thing collecting is all about."

"Have you been collecting for a long time, sir?" asked Miles.

"Yes, I have. In fact, far longer than any of you have been alive."

The actor paused in order to set the Bible upon an antique-style reading table beside his chair.

"But I don't just collect coins. As you can see, I also collect books. And I love to collect rare stamps. I have an 'Inverted Jenny,' a rare 1918 stamp that pictures a military bi-plane. Due to a printing mistake, a few stamps accidently had the image of the plane upside down. I'll tell you, it is worth a small fortune. I had to go to great lengths to get my hands on that stamp."

"Do you often have to go to great lengths to get a rare stamp," Zayne asked without expression, "*or* a rare coin?"

For a moment Mr. Evers hesitated, wondering if Zayne's question might be implying something. However after studying the boy, Mr. Evers relaxed.

"Yes," he continued. "Sometimes it takes years of hard work to finally get my hands on a prized collectible."

"Mr. Evers," said Miles, "did you know that such a rare 'tribute penny' was here in town."

"I had no idea," the gentleman answered casually, "until the stories came out in the paper."

Tomas, who had begun taking notes, stopped and asked, "How do you think a coin like that could have wound up here?"

"I'm not sure. I suppose a collector might have lost it. I'm just glad it ended up in my hands." After saying this, Mr. Evers caught himself. "Of course, I'm sorry if that was the case. But since they didn't claim it, and it went up for auction, I'm grateful to be the *legal* owner."

All of the investigators noticed how Mr. Evers emphasized the word 'legal.'

"I think the police wondered if the coin might have been stolen," Miles followed up. "Do you think that's possible?"

"Stolen?" the famous actor replied, momentarily averting his eyes. "No, I don't think the coin was stolen. How would a stolen coin end up in the middle of the sidewalk?"

"Mr. Evers, do you happen to know which store the coin was found in front of?" wondered Zayne.

Once again, the old man paused to look Zayne over. Zayne returned an innocent smile.

"Which store?" he finally replied. "Let me think. It has been such a long time since I read those newspaper articles. And the truth is, I don't do any of my own shopping, so I never go down to Main Street. My housekeeper picks up my groceries and my medicines and such. Uh, well, let me see. I believe the boy found the coin in front of a hardware store. There *is* a little hardware store down on Main Street, right? Yes, that was it, the hardware store."

"No, sir," Tomas politely corrected him, "it was actually found in front of the dry cleaners."

"Oh, was it?" the actor said, fidgeting a bit in his seat. "I had forgotten. Is the location important for some reason?"

"Maybe," answered Miles, "there had been some rumors about stolen coins being sold by the owner of the dry cleaners."

"Really," Mr. Evers replied, appearing quite surprised. "I hadn't heard that."

"Yes," Zayne added. "Back then some suspicious people had been seen coming in and out of Mr. Gruber's dry cleaning shop."

"No, son," Mr. Evers corrected, "Mr. Gruber runs the pharmacy. It's Mr. Miller who owns the dry cleaners."

"I believe you're right, sir," Zayne said courteously. "But, if I may ask, how did you know that? I thought you never went down to Main Street."

"I, well, uh," the actor stammered, completely caught off guard. "I guess I have picked up the names of the shopkeepers over the years." Quickly regaining his composure, Mr. Evers reached for a gold bell that rested on the reading table, picked it up, and rang it. "Now I think it's time that you kids got a look at this famous coin," he said, placing the gold bell back on the table.

Within moments, the butler appeared at the doorway.

"You rang, sir," he asked in his typically formal way.

"Yes. Would you please bring me the tribute penny? I have some young guests who I think might enjoy seeing it."

"Right away, sir."

Five minutes later, after each investigator had put on a pair of latex gloves, Mr. Evers was carefully handing Miles the famous coin.

After looking it over, Miles passed it on to Grant, who eventually passed it on to Tomas, who finally passed it on to Zayne.

"Cool," Tomas had exclaimed during his turn, "that's *the* coin."

Mr. Evers, who now held the coin once again, began to speak.

"Obviously, you noticed Tiberius on the front, but on the back…" He flipped the coin over. "…on the back is the inscription 'Pontif Maxim' which declared Tiberius to be the head of the Roman religion."

"Who is the woman on the back?" inquired Grant, speaking for the first time.

"That is believed to be Livia, Tiberius' mother. She is holding a laurel branch, a symbol of peace."

"Thank you so much for showing it to us," Miles declared.

"Certainly," Mr. Evers answered as he placed the coin back into a small sealable bag. "Is there anything else I can do for you before you go?"

"There is one thing," Zayne replied, digging his hand deep into his front pocket and pulling out a plastic case and a pen. "I do some collecting too, and I've got an original *Hollywood Hayseeds'* trading card. Would you mind if I have your autograph?"

While Zayne's friends rolled their eyes, the actor smiled and said, "not at all."

Zayne opened the case and removed the trading card. Next, he handed both the card and the pen to Mr. Evers, who signed it with the beautiful flowing signature of a man who had given many, many autographs. Then, he returned the card to Zayne. Finally, Zayne placed it back in the case and put the case back in his pocket.

As Mr. Evers and the children left the library and returned to the entryway, Zayne spoke up once more.

"Oh, yeah," he said, "I almost forgot to ask you something. Mr. Evers, why did you dress up as your character from *The Hollywood*

Hayseeds when you visited Mr. Gruber down at the pharmacy? And, why did you continue to do it each time you visited the Townsends during your attempts to buy the coin from them?"

Everyone stopped dead in their tracks.

Miles, Grant, and Tomas stared at Zayne with their mouths open wide. They each expected Mr. Evers to lose his temper at such a bold accusation. However, he didn't. Instead, a slow grin appeared on his face, which was followed by a slight shaking of his head.

"I had a suspicion about you, young man," Mr. Evers finally said. "Wait here, I'll be right back."

Several minutes later, a man wearing old work pants, a thread-bare coat, and a tattered fedora entered the room. As he approached, the four friends barely recognized Mr. Evers.

"Howdy, ya'll," he said with a country twang in his voice.

Zayne reached back into his pocket and got out his autographed trading card. The picture on the card had come to life before them.

Evers removed his hat and began to speak, once again using his normal voice.

"I did visit Mr. Gruber all those years ago," he confessed. "And, I did visit the Townsend family in an effort to buy the coin."

"But why the disguise?" asked Tomas in amazement.

"For one reason, because the tribute penny could very easily have been stolen. And although I wanted it very much, Jess Evers has a reputation to uphold. It wouldn't do to be associated with stolen property." The old actor removed the fedora hat and held it with both hands. "I know all about Frank Miller. Through some back door channels, he had even tried to sell me some coins, which to my credit I did not buy. But I knew where the young boy had discovered the coin, and like the police, I suspected what it might mean. However, finding a tribute penny of such pristine quality was something I simply couldn't pass up. So what was I to do? I went after the coin, but not as Jess Evers." He placed the hat back upon his head. "Instead, my dear old character from *The Hollywood Hayseeds* went in my place. To my great luck and surprise, neither Mr. Gruber nor Mrs. Townsend recognized me."

"Mr. Evers," Miles began, "when we spoke with Mr. Gruber, he got the impression you believed that there might be more coins out there somewhere? Is that true?"

A long silence passed as the actor weighed his words carefully.

"Mr. Gruber was correct," he finally answered. "I did believe that more priceless coins might be found. In fact, I still believe it."

"You think there are more lost coins?" Tomas proclaimed, his eyes growing wide. "Here in town?"

"I'm sorry, I can't say more," replied Mr. Evers, once again removing the hat and holding it in front of himself with both hands. "I've said too much already. Besides, I'm not even sure. It's just a theory. I looked into it myself, for years, in fact. But I'm too old now, and if I'm right, it might present some, uh, complications for me. So, I've given up the treasure hunting. You kids are clever. Keep searching. Who knows, you might find that you're onto something bigger than you ever imagined."

With that, Mr. Evers said his goodbyes and sent the investigators on their way.

As the four friends began to make their way down the mansion's long winding driveway, Tomas spoke first.

"Did he actually use the word treasure?"

The others nodded excitedly.

"Can you believe it?" Miles burst as he rhythmically pushed the wheels on his chair. "Can you believe that Jess Evers just told us all of that, including his confession about dressing up and visiting Mr. Gruber and the Townsends?" Then turning his head toward Zayne, he asked quizzically, "But how did you know?"

"I knew before we got here," Zayne said simply. "At least, I was pretty sure, ever since Chief told us that an interview with Mr. Evers should be our next step. He suspected that Mr. Evers had been the mysterious visitor, for the description sounded too much like a character from *The Hollywood Hayseeds* to be a mere coincidence. Why else would Chief suggest that we see Evers? If he was nothing more than the current owner of the coin, what new information would he have to offer? Besides, Evers pretty much gave himself away. One minute he said that he didn't ever go shopping on Main Street, and the next minute he corrects me about the names of the shopkeepers."

"I thought that was strange," nodded Tomas.

"Children wait," came a voice from behind.

As they turned, the butler came running down the drive. Upon reaching them, and after taking a minute to try and catch his breath, he spoke.

"Mr. Evers wanted me to give you this."

He handed a folded piece of paper to Grant, bowed slightly, turned, and began the walk back up to the house.

Grant unfolded the paper as the others gathered around him.

"What does it say?" Miles pleaded.

"April or May of the year before," Grant read. "Rain o so."

"Rain or snow?" inquired Tomas, straining to try and get a glimpse of the words.

"No," Grant shook his head. "It says 'Rain o so.'"

106

Having been impressed by his earlier cleverness, the others looked to Zayne.

"What's that supposed to mean?" Tomas asked him.

For quite some time, Zayne stared at the paper in his friend's large hands. Finally, with a perplexed look on his face, he replied, "I have absolutely no idea."

Chapter Ten

Tomas was supposed to be asleep. Instead, he was lying in bed, wide awake, staring at the ceiling.

The clock read ten-thirty. Six hours had passed since he, Miles, Grant and Zayne had left the house of Jess Evers. Three hours had passed since he left Declan's house, where all of the Bible Club had met to discuss the interview with the famous actor.

Everyone had been shocked by the revelation that Mr. Evers was the mysterious stranger that visited both the Townsends and Mr. Gruber. Everyone had been stunned that Zayne confronted Evers so boldly. And, everyone had been excited by both the possibility of more lost coins and the old gentleman's cryptic message.

April or May of the year before. Rain o so.

The entire group had agreed that Mr. Evers was trying to give them a clue, but what did it mean? Declan had suggested that it might be some kind of coded message. It seemed reasonable, but if so, they had no idea how to decode it. After various unproductive theories, Talia had brought the conversation new direction.

"For a moment, let's stop trying to figure out what it means," she had offered, "and instead try to figure out why he gave it to us."

There were two possibilities, they had concluded. First, Mr. Evers had hinted at a treasure. Perhaps he really had given up the search, deciding to pass on to them some information about how to find it. Second, Mr. Evers had been concerned that the coin, or coins, had been stolen. Maybe he knew it to be true but couldn't say anything because of the complications he had referenced during their interview. In that case, his message might be about the theft.

"I think the second idea is the most likely," Miles had said. "In my opinion, he seemed to know that the coins were stolen. And the message is too short to be some kind of treasure map."

Now lying in bed and pondering the earlier conversation, Tomas agreed with Miles. He then tried to continue the train of thought that his friend had begun so much earlier in the evening.

"Okay, if the message is about the coin being stolen then what was Mr. Evers trying to say? Zayne had suggested that 'April or May of the year before' may be a clue to *when* the crime occurred. That makes sense, but what about the rest?" He rolled onto his side and found himself staring at his lamp. "What does 'Rain o so' mean?" he wondered. "Abigail suggested that it might be *where* the crime occurred. That makes sense too, but 'Rain o so' isn't the name of any kind of place that I've ever heard of." He rolled the other way and faced the wall on which he and his dad had taped a world map.

As his eyes drifted to the familiar borders of Mexico, a thought struck him like a thunderbolt. Amidst his sudden excitement, Tomas tried to quickly sit upright in bed. However he had been too close to the edge, and he fell onto the floor with a loud thud. Untangling himself from his blanket, Tomas jumped up and turned on his bedroom light. A second later, he was standing at the wall, rapidly scanning Mexico on the map.

"Only the state capitals are named," he exclaimed in despair.

Just then, his bedroom door opened.

"Was that you making that racket, hijo?" his father asked him. "What are you doing awake at this hour?"

"Papi," Tomas begged, "what is the name of the city where Abu was born?"

Caught off guard by the unexpected question, Tomas' father hesitated momentarily before answering.

"Uh, your grandfather was born in Reynosa, why?"

Tomas' face lit up.

"Where is Reynosa, Papi?"

"Right about here," his father said, pointed to a spot on the map where Mexico and Texas met.

"Papi, 'Rain o so' is Reynosa. It's Reynosa, Mexico. I bet that's what Mr. Evers meant, but he didn't know how to spell it. That's it. That has to be it. The coin was stolen in Reynosa, Mexico in April or May the year before Alex Townsend found it on the sidewalk. I have to tell the others. Wait, I can't, they're all in bed. I don't believe it. I figured it out. At least, I think I've figured it out."

"Hijo," his father said with a confused look, "I have no idea what you are talking about. But, I'm tired. Tell me about it in the morning. And go to bed."

"Yes Papi," Tomas answered as his father closed his bedroom door.

Tomas turned out his light and climbed back in bed, but his heart was racing with excitement. In fact, he couldn't fall asleep until well after midnight.

The next morning, Tomas got up at seven. He was tired and it showed. Large dark circles had formed under his eyes, and his parents noticed. "You look exhausted, hijo," his Dad said with concern. "Why are you up so early?"

"Reynosa, Papi, Reynosa," he replied. "I have to find out if I'm right about the message that the famous actor from *The Hollywood Hayseeds* gave us. His message told us when and where the Roman coin had been stolen, I just know it."

"Hijo," said his father as he took his lunch out of the refrigerator, "you said something very much like that last night, and I didn't understand a word you were talking about then. And, I don't understand a word you are talking about now." He picked up a thermos of coffee from the kitchen counter. "I've got to get to work. Explain all of this Roman coin and Reynosa stuff to me when I get home, okay?"

With that, Tomas' father kissed his wife good-bye and headed out the back door.

"Hijito," his mother said, turning her attention to Tomas, "why don't you go back to bed? You look so tired."

"Mama, I can't. This is muy importante. I need to get down to the library as soon as it opens."

"Alright, little one," she answered, "but have a nice breakfast first. Will you be at the library all day again, like you were before? Do you need me to pack you a lunch?"

"Yes, Mama."

Ten minutes later, Tomas had finished getting dressed, scarfed down his breakfast, and placed both the Case File and his lunch in a backpack. After dashing out into the garage, he was soon on his bike and peddling his way to the library. As he zoomed down street after street, Tomas wished he could have told his friends about his idea, but he wasn't sure they would be awake yet. He decided he would call them later. Right now, filled from head to toe with excitement, Tomas had to get started searching for the proof that would validate his theory.

At ten minutes until eight, Tomas arrived at the library, but the doors didn't open until the top of the hour. He didn't feel like he could wait.

Needing to spend some nervous energy, Tomas began pacing back and forth on the sidewalk.

"It's just got to be the when and where of the coin robbery," he thought to himself. "Mr. Evers knows that it was stolen. And he was trying to tell us, without directly telling us. But what were the complications he spoke about? Well, if the coin had been stolen, could Mr. Evers get in trouble? No, I don't think so. He simply bought it at an auction. There isn't anything illegal about that. Wait. Would he have to return the coin to the rightful owner? It would be stolen property. Maybe he would have to give it back. And he certainly doesn't want to lose his tribute penny. All of that makes sense, but we still need proof. I've got to find some evidence. I've got to find an article that tells about a coin robbery in Reynosa."

At that moment, a young woman could be seen inside the library approaching the front door. Then, with the twist of an Allen wrench, the doors were unlocked, and Tomas burst inside.

"Good morning, Tomas," the young woman greeted. A reference librarian, she had helped Tomas and his friends on their previous visit. "I'm surprised to see you this early. Are you here to do more research on that coin?"

"Good morning, Ms. Holliday," Tomas answered. "Yes, I am. I think I may have figured out something that might help us. May I have a study room? And may I have a password to log onto a computer?"

"Of course you may," she smiled. "Let me get you a key to a room and one of the papers with a password."

She walked Tomas over to the reference area, opened the drawer to her desk, and removed both a key and a slip of paper.

"You know where everything is, if you need help let me know."

"Actually, I do need help."

Tomas told Ms. Holliday about the message from Mr. Evers and about his idea regarding its meaning.

"That's a pretty good theory," she said thoughtfully. "If you don't speak the language, Reynosa could easily turn into 'rain o so.' It sounds like you are going to need a Mexican news database. I think we have access to one, but the articles will all probably be in Spanish. Do you know Spanish, Tomas?"

"My mom and dad were born in Mexico," he answered. "I'm not fluent, but I read it pretty well. I think I should be able to understand."

"Great," she answered warmly, "why don't you set your stuff down in the study room, and then I'll help you get started with that database."

Tomas walked to the study rooms as Ms. Holliday headed over to the computers.

After unlocking the door, he placed the room's key in his pocket. Then, he carefully removed the Case File from his backpack and laid it on the circular table. Flipping to the back of the binder, Tomas removed several blank pieces of paper for note taking. Next, after grabbing a pencil from the front pouch, he hung the backpack over a seat back. As he began to leave the room, pulling the door closed behind him, Tomas stopped and quickly checked his pocket. He wanted to make sure that he still had the key. The study room doors locked automatically, and during his previous visit he had accidently locked himself out, needing to ask Ms. Holliday to allow him back in.

After the short walk to the computer area, Tomas joined Ms. Holliday at a work station.

"Okay, this is the database I was telling you about," Ms. Holliday said. "It's filled exclusively with articles from Latin American newspapers. That would be an overwhelming amount of information, but you can limit your search by selecting 'Mexico' here." She pointed to an area on the computer monitor. "And in this search box," she added, touching another portion of the screen, "you can enter the keywords you're looking for. I would try 'Reynosa robbery' or 'Reynosa crime.' It will bring up a long list of articles, just like your searches last week. However," she paused as she moved her finger across the monitor, "you can narrow down the dates of the articles here on this side. Do you have any questions?"

"No, I think that makes sense."

"Alright. Well, good luck. Let me know if you need any more help."

For the better part of the next four hours, Tomas searched the database. It felt like he had read every article about every crime that ever happened in Reynosa. Still, there had been nothing mentioning the theft of any coins. Discouraged and ready to give up on his theory, Tomas slumped back in his chair. Following a sigh, he then prayed silently to himself.

"God, I don't know what to do. Even if I'm right, I could search forever and never find anything. Please help me. Amen."

When he had finished praying a thought suddenly occurred to him. With a curious expression, Tomas looked up to the ceiling as if trying to see into heaven.

"Well, what do I have to lose," he said out loud while sitting upright and beginning to type.

Reynosa atraco a un banco, he typed.

Then, he set the time parameters of the database and pressed enter.

One article appeared.

"I haven't seen this one," Tomas thought, rather surprised, and he began to read.

"Robo del banco…caja de seguridad…magnate de los negocios…recientement fallecido…el coleccionista…un desconocido fugado…el sospechoso de Americano…objetos robados…"

Amazed, Tomas leaned closer to the screen.

"What was taken?" he asked himself, scanning the document.

"…objetos robados…monedas romanas de inestimable…homenaje centavo…"

For a moment Tomas couldn't breathe. He stared wide-eyed at the computer screen. Could it really be? He read the words again. Yes, there was no mistaking it.

Tomas didn't know what to do. He got up. He sat back down. He got up again.

"I need to…I need to print," he decided. With shaking hands, he dragged the computer mouse and selected the print command.

Quickly, he logged himself off the computer. Then he raced over to the printer.

"Come on, come on," Tomas said impatiently as he waited for the printer to warm-up. When the printer finally spat out his article, he grabbed it. Half-walking and half-running, he began making his way toward the study room.

Ms. Holliday spotted him.

"What's all the excitement Tomas? Did you find your evidence?" she asked.

"Yes ma'am, I did," he answered back, an enormous grin upon his face.

"Congratulations!"

Tomas said 'thank you' as he disappeared behind a bookshelf.

After making his way through a maze of books, Tomas soon found himself back at his study room. He stopped dead in his tracks. There on the other side of the study room's window stood Zayne. The room was sound proof, but Tomas could read Zayne's lips as his friend moved his mouth in a slow, exaggerated sentence.

"I AM LOCKED INSIDE," Zayne mouthed, pointing rapidly at the door knob.

Since the door only locked on the outside, Tomas didn't understand how that could be. He reached into his pocket and pulled out the key. He then tried to push the key into the door's lock, but it would only go halfway and no more. After several failed attempts, Tomas looked at Zayne and shrugged his shoulders.

"GO GET HELP," Zayne seemed to be saying, now pointing toward the front of the library.

It took nearly twenty minutes for the library custodian to free Zayne from his prison.

"What happened?" Tomas asked his friend as Ms. Holliday and the custodian listened in.

"Well," Zayne said in his matter of fact tone, "I stopped by your house early this morning and your mom said that you had left for the library. So I came down and looked for you in the study rooms. Then I saw your backpack in there, but the door was locked. Anyway, since we are investigators now, I've begun carrying around some tiny screwdrivers. What I mean is, in all of the detective books, there is always someone who knows how to pick a lock. And, well, I figured I'd better learn how to do it. It worked too. I only needed fifteen tries. Unfortunately, I must have broken something off inside the lock, because after I got in, I couldn't get back out."

"How long were you in there?" Ms. Holliday asked with alarm.

"About an hour and a half. I'm very sorry about the lock, Ms. Holliday."

"That's okay, Zayne," she chuckled. "I'm just glad we were able to get you out."

As Ms. Holliday and the custodian walked away, Zayne asked Tomas what he had been doing all morning. Tomas' answer spewed out like lava from a volcano.

"Zayne, I figured out Mr. Evers' message, and I've got it."

"Got what?" Zayne wondered.

"I've got the proof that the coin was stolen!"

Chapter Eleven

As he looked through the pantry, Zayne's arms were already overflowing with snacks. He had pretzels, chips, popcorn, and three varieties of crackers. When he tried to add the fudge cookies, he nearly dropped his entire load but somehow managed to make it work. Unable to fit anything else into his arms, yet still not willing to overlook the tortillas, Zayne took hold of the bag with his teeth.

Declan couldn't believe his eyes as he walked into the kitchen.

"Wooks good, huh?" Zayne mumbled to Declan; the tortilla bag preventing him from opening his mouth as he spoke.

"Zayne," Declan scolded, "when Chief said we could help ourselves to some snacks, I don't think he meant *all* the snacks."

Zayne dropped his load upon the kitchen's pass through counter. He then stuck his head through the opening that led to the living room. "Hey guys," he shouted, "there's plenty of food. Come help yourself." Turning his attention back to Declan, he said, "Ah, Chief won't mind. He always lets me eat his food."

"I'm not so sure that he lets you eat his food," Declan countered. "I just don't think he knows how to stop you."

"He still has his gun," joked Zayne while beginning to scavenge through the refrigerator.

Earlier in the day, Tomas had called for an urgent meeting of the Bible Club. He had teased his friends with the promise of 'Big News.' Chief couldn't attend for he had to be at the church, but he gave permission for his young friends to use the house.

"Oh my goodness," Zayne declared as he peered into the refrigerator, "jackpot!"

After reaching deep into the back, Zayne pulled something out of the fridge and turned toward Declan. Then, the redhead thrust a can of spray whipped cream into the air like a champion holding a trophy. His eyes were dancing, and he had a smile from one ear to the other.

"There's no pie or anything," said Declan. "What are you going to put that on?"

"I'm not going to put it on anything. I'm just going to eat it."

"Plain?!? That's disgusting. Anyway, just hurry up. Everyone else is ready, and I want to hear what Tomas has to say."

Using a bowl from the cupboard, Zayne shook the can of whipped cream, turned it upside down and began to spray.

"Did you know," he said as the mound of whipped cream continued to grow, "that they use nitrous oxide to propel the cream out of these cans. That's the same gas they use at the dentist's office when you need a cavity filled or a tooth pulled. Isn't that funny?"

Mesmerized as the mound of whip cream in Zayne's bowl slowly became a mountain, Declan offered no reply.

"Don't you get it? In this whipping cream, nitrous oxide helps *give* cavities. Later, the nitrous oxide helps *treat* cavities. Funny right?"

"Just hurry up," Declan cried as he left the kitchen.

Soon everyone found their familiar seats around Chief's living room, including Grace. Although she hadn't been an active participant, Grace was constantly pestering her big sister for updates about the investigation. So, Abigail thought it would be much easier to bring her along rather than try to explain it all to her later.

Typically when the Bible Club gathered, everyone directed their focus toward the leather recliner at the head of the circle, but not tonight. Tonight, all eyes were fixed a bit to the right, where Tomas sat crisscross upon the floor. All eyes, that is, except for Zayne's. His focus was on the whipped cream that he had begun ferociously scooping into his mouth.

With the Case File open upon his lap, Tomas waited to speak while Abigail got the meeting started.

"So we've apparently had some major developments since last we met," she began. "Tomas, will you tell us all about what you've discovered?"

"Well," he began, suddenly feeling a bit shy with the spotlight cast upon him, "I think everyone has heard by now that I figured out Mr. Evers' message. However, what you might not know is that I have also found evidence that the Roman coin was stolen." Everyone gasped with surprise. Everyone except for Zayne, who already knew the big announcement, and who seemed so busy with his whipped cream that he didn't appear to be paying attention.

"You're kidding!" exclaimed Abigail, half jumping off the couch. "Tell us all about it."

Tomas then went on to recount the story of how, while lying in bed, the idea of Reynosa occurred to him. He then described the morning he spent at the library searching through the Latin American news database, explaining that after four hours he still hadn't found anything new.

"I was ready to give up," he told his friends, "but I said a quick prayer. Suddenly, and I'm not making this up, I got an idea for a search. And it was exactly what we've been looking for."

Tomas unsnapped the Case File's binding and pulled out a piece of paper with a news article carefully taped upon it. After snapping the binder shut again, he held the article up for everyone to see.

"Tell us what it says," Miles asked excitedly.

"Well, my Spanish isn't perfect, but I'll do my best to translate," said Tomas.

Yesterday, a terrible crime took place when the Central Bank of Reynosa was robbed. The bank robbery appeared to target only a single safety deposit box. The box belonged to...

Tomas paused, and said, "I think this next part means 'big businessman' or maybe 'shipping tycoon' or something like that, but I'm not exactly sure." He continued.

The box belonged to shipping tycoon Javier Diaz. The recently deceased millionaire was known throughout the world for his antiques and collectibles. At approximately eleven thirty in the morning, the criminal pulled a gun on the bank teller and demanded access to the safety deposit boxes. Once inside, the thief used a small amount of...

"I think this means 'plastic explosives.'"

...plastic explosives to blow open the door to Mr. Diaz's safety deposit box. He then left through the rear of the bank. The police did not arrive in time to stop him. Although he wore a mask, the unknown fugitive is thought to be from the United States. Police also believe that the American suspect fled over the border into Texas. The stolen objects include Spanish doubloons, early Egyptian coins, and Roman coins known as tribute pennies. If you have any information about this robbery, please contact police headquarters.

"Wow!" exclaimed Talia.

"Wow is right," seconded Miles. "It even says tribute penny."

"No," said Declan, "it doesn't say tribute penny. It says tribute pennies, which means there are probably more coins out there somewhere."

"Which means," added Abigail, "that Mr. Evers probably knew about this when Alex found the coin."

Turning toward Abigail, Talia asked, "Why do you say that?"

"It explains his behavior."

Abigail rose to her feet and assumed the posture of a teacher before her class.

"Just after Alex finds the coin," she continued, "Mr. Evers dresses as his character from *The Hollywood Hayseeds* and visits Mr. Gruber. By his own admission, he dressed up because he thought the coin might be stolen, and he didn't want people to know of his interest in stolen property. He claims that the location of the coin's discovery caused him to believe this..."

"That seems reasonable," Talia interrupted, "given Mr. Miller's reputation and Evers' story that Miller once tried to sell him fenced coins."

"I agree," replied Abigail. "However, Mr. Gruber thought Evers was looking for multiple coins, which Evers admitted. Why would finding one tribute penny outside of Miller's dry cleaners lead you to believe there might be more coins? It doesn't add up. No, the most obvious explanation is that Evers knew about the theft in Mexico from the beginning."

"How?" asked Tomas.

Having finished his whipped cream, Zayne loudly dropped his spoon into his bowl. Unfortunately, he did not realize that a large dab of the cream had gotten onto the end of his nose.

"My theory," offered Zayne, having taken an interest in the conversation for the first time, "is that, as a fellow collector, he was aware of the theft in Reynosa. But because it happened in Mexico, our police department was not."

"Why would he have kept that to himself all these years?" wondered Grant.

"So he could find the coins and add them to his own collection," Talia frowned. "If the police knew they were stolen, Mr. Evers wouldn't be able to have them."

"If he found them," added a cross-eyed Zayne, who was staring at the newly discovered cream on his nose.

"Hasn't Mr. Evers committed some kind of crime like withholding evidence or something?" asked Miles.

"I don't think so," Declan answered, shaking his head. "Unless, of course, being selfish is a crime."

"If being selfish were a crime," said Grant to no one in particular, "then we'd all be guilty."

"In a spiritual sense, it is," Abigail replied, "and we are all guilty. That's why we need Jesus."

A thoughtful look passed over Grant's face.

"Well, where do we go next?" wondered Tomas as he put the article back in the Case File.

The room went silent.

After some time, Zayne, who had now cleaned the whipped cream off his nose, spoke up.

"We don't have a treasure map, so we can't go searching for the remaining coins. And we don't know anything about the criminal who committed the robbery in Mexico, so that's a dead end, at least for now. Therefore, the only reasonable road is the one we are already on. We must discover how that Roman coin ended up on the sidewalk. If we know that, we might have a firm connection to the crime in Mexico and perhaps even some information about the location of the other coins."

"Spot on," said Talia. "But how do we do it? Frank Miller isn't going to tell us anything."

More silence followed, for everyone knew Talia was right.

"I wish we could find the dancing girl," suggested Abigail, half to herself.

Grace, who had been patiently listening to the entire conversation, looked at her sister and asked, "What dancing girl?"

"Just before finding the coin, Alex Townsend saw a girl dancing on the sidewalk," Abigail replied. "But there is no way we could ever find her."

"If she even existed," Miles added. "Remember, Alex doesn't really have any memory of it. His mom only says that he mentioned it once in a police interview."

"So we're stuck?" offered Declan dejectedly.

"Unless Frank Miller is going to talk to us," answered Zayne, "and I have no idea why he would. Then, yes, it appears as if we are stuck."

At that moment, the front door opened and closed, followed by the approaching sound of halting footsteps.

"Hello," greeted Chief after appearing in the living room. "How's it going?"

"Good and bad," Miles answered.

"Well, let me get a cup of coffee and you can tell me all about it."

Chief dropped his keys into a dish on a console table and then disappeared into the kitchen. After a few minutes had passed, he reemerged with a large steaming mug of coffee.

"So," Chief began as he carefully lowered himself into his recliner, "I'm assuming this is about your investigation into the Roman coin. Tell me the latest. Both the good and the bad. But before you do, I saw my can of whipped cream in the garbage. Did you guys bring a pie or something? If so, I'd love a piece."

"There's no pie," answered Abigail.

"What did you use the whipped cream for then? I didn't have any ice cream."

Everyone stared at Zayne and his empty bowl.

Following their gaze, Chief looked at Zayne and then down at his bowl.

"You didn't?" Chief asked.

Zayne smiled sheepishly.

"You did," Chief gasped. "Plain?!? That's disgusting." After shaking his head in disbelief, Chief tried to refocus.

"Okay," he said, unable to stop himself from taking another quick look at Zayne's empty bowl, "back to the investigation."

For the next few minutes, the Bible Club told Chief the good news about Tomas' discovery and the bad news about their apparent dead end.

"I'll tell you this," Chief said when his young friends had finished, "that's some fine detective work. A heist in Mexico, huh? That explains why we couldn't trace the coin. And I agree, it sounds like Evers knew about it from the beginning but chose to keep quiet. So there were more coins out there somewhere. Amazing! I wonder if they're still missing. Now that we know about the Mexico angle, I'll talk with my friends at the police department and have them see what ever came of it all. Was anyone ever caught? Did the coins ever get returned? But other than that, I'm afraid you're right. Unless you can somehow connect the coin on the street to Frank Miller, there just doesn't seem to be anywhere else to go. Don't be too disappointed though, you've done a great job!"

Later that evening, as the members of the Bible Club left Chief's house, there was a sense of both joy and sadness. Joy in the fact that they had taken a closed twenty-year-old investigation and given it new life. Sadness because they had taken a closed twenty-year-old investigation and given it new life, yet there didn't seem to be anything else that they could do.

As the group walked home together, they were left hoping that some unexpected development might allow them to continue the case. For now, they said their goodnights and each went their separate ways. Everyone, that is, except Miles and Grant, who lived in the same neighborhood.

At first, the two friends went along silently, for Grant seemed to be in a reflective mood. Besides, Miles strongly suspected what consumed Grant's thoughts, and he didn't want to press him.

Finally, however, the silence was broken when Grant asked if he could help push Miles up a steep patch of sidewalk. Miles said, "Yes, thank you," and then decided to try and probe the depths.

"You seem thoughtful tonight," Miles began as Grant took the handles of the wheelchair. "But it isn't about the Roman coin, is it?"

"No," replied Grant, "it's about becoming a Christian."

"I suspected as much. Have you thought more about what Chief told you? Do you believe that Jesus really is the Son of God?"

"Yes," answered Grant. "Or, at least I think so. Well, I don't know. I think I think so…if that makes any sense. Clearly, Jesus is one of a kind. I could see that in his answers to the Sadducees and the Pharisees. But being the Son of God is more than just being unique. It means that Jesus was the most unique person that ever lived."

"I agree. However, you don't think he was the most unique person ever."

"Yes…no…maybe."

Once more, they went on in silence until they reached the top of the hill. There, Grant let go of the handles and came around to the front of Miles' wheelchair in order to talk face to face.

"It was funny tonight," Grant resumed. "Do you remember when I said, 'if being selfish were a crime then we'd all be guilty'?'"

Miles nodded.

"Then Abigail basically said, 'we are all guilty, and that's why Jesus came.' Her words stung."

"Why," asked Miles, "did you think she was showing you up?"

"No, not at all. Her words stung because I am selfish. The other night, Chief talked about the sin problem and how it keeps us from being in a good relationship with God. And I understood what he meant. However, I understood what he meant as an idea. I understood in my head, you know what I mean? But it is a much different thing to admit in your heart. Sure, I'm a sinner. I guess I can agree with that. Yet being willing to admit that Jesus had to come for me…to die for me…because of *my* sin…well, that's a lot harder. And suddenly, when Abigail said that, I could see…for the first time, I think…that I need a Savior."

Miles gently pushed back, "Well, aren't you really saying that it's time to become a Christian?"

Grant looked up into the night sky.

"I don't know," he continued. "Maybe I do believe Jesus is the Son of God, or at least that he could be, but didn't Chief say that you have to choose to follow him…to make him the leader of your life?"

"Yes," Miles answered softly.

"Even if I could find the faith," Grant said, "even if I could let go of my doubts and questions, I still don't know if I could let him be my leader."

"Why not?"

"Expectations, Miles, expectations. Everyone, everywhere has expectations for me: my parents, my coaches, and everyone else I meet. I'm the superstar athlete. I'm supposed to play the sports, win the games, earn a free ride to college, and make it to the big time."

"I thought you didn't really like sports all that much?" Miles asked.

"I don't. At least, not as much as I'm supposed to. There's so much pressure all the time that it really isn't all that much fun."

"So what's the problem?"

"Well," Grant paused, fighting back tears, "I can't let Jesus be the leader of my life because He might want me to give up the sports. He might want me to go against everyone's expectations. Jesus might have an entirely different plan for my life and that might mean letting everyone else down. He might do that, right? Jesus might ask me to do something that contradicts what everyone else is pushing me to do, right?"

"Yes," Miles said simply.

Grant turned his back to his friend and whispered, "I can't. I can't do it. I can't risk letting all of those people down. I just can't let go."

Resuming the silence, they continued their journey home.

When they had reached Miles' house, he said 'goodnight' to Grant and began to roll himself up his driveway. But he suddenly stopped.

Spinning around and facing his friend, Miles quietly said, "Grant."

"Yes, Miles."

"When you said, 'everyone has expectations for you,' did that include me?"

Grant smiled. "No," he said, "that didn't include you. That's why you're my best friend."

"Good. Thanks, Grant. You're my best friend too. Goodnight."

"Goodnight, Miles."

As Grant continued his walk home, the smile on his face remained, and a single tear rolled down his cheek.

Chapter Twelve

A few of the children were finishing their snacks. Most, however, had left the side room and were playing a game of tag in the large center room.

Grace was doing neither.

Instead, she sat alone, staring at the clock.

"What's the matter, Grace?" asked Mrs. Elliott, Grace's teacher for *Wednesday Night Kids Night* at church.

"I'm bored," sulked Grace, propping her head up with both hands. "Katie and Malia didn't come tonight, and I have nothing to do. What time are we finished?"

"Sorry, Grace," answered Mrs. Elliott as she knelt down to look the young girl in the eyes. "The lesson was short and we still have about fifteen minutes before the parents start arriving. Don't you want to play tag?"

"Not really."

"Hmm. Well, you could go over and help your sister out in the toddler room."

"No thanks," replied Grace. "Last time I did that little Timmy Wilson bit me. I still have his teeth marks on my arm." Grace held her left arm out for inspection. "See. Abigail said that I would have Timmy's teeth marks on me for the rest of my life. Is that true?"

Mrs. Elliott smiled.

"No, Grace," she said, "I don't think so. I have an idea. Why don't you draw me a picture? You're a wonderful artist."

"Okay, but I don't know what to draw."

"Let's see," Mrs. Elliott replied, scratching her head. "Why don't you draw me a picture that tells an interesting story? When you're done, I'll try to guess what it's about?"

Grace was a terrific artist, and she did love to draw, so the suggestion of creating a picture for a guessing game proved to be a winner.

"Okay," Grace declared, having completely forgotten her boredom. "You'll get three guesses."

With that, Grace dashed off to collect some paper and markers.

Just a few minutes later, Grace slapped a marker down upon the table and declared, "I'm finished."

Mrs. Elliott, who had been cleaning up the snacks, replied, "Be right there."

After disposing of some used napkins, plates, and cups, she came over and sat beside Grace.

"Alright, let me figure out your story," Mrs. Elliott said, carefully examining the picture. "Wow. It's very well done. Here's a girl…on a sidewalk…she is…hmm…doing hopscotch. Is that a school building behind her? And, what's this on the sidewalk here? It looks like a gold coin…or is it a marble? Now, there's a boy too. He seems to be watching the girl."

"You have to take a guess now," Grace stated firmly.

"Well, this is a girl at school playing hopscotch while a friend watches."

"Nope," responded Grace happily, "try again."

Mrs. Elliott looked over the picture once more.

"Okay, the girl isn't playing hopscotch," Mrs. Elliott said to herself.

"I know," she finally declared, "she's dancing."

"Is that your guess?" asked Grace.

"Yes."

"Well, your right about the dancing, but what about the boy? And where is she? And what's that on the ground? You just have to be more specific."

Following a long pause, Mrs. Elliott clarified her second guess.

"Well those buildings remind me of downtown. So, I'll say that she is dancing on the sidewalk downtown, and the little boy is just watching."

"Good," smiled Grace, "but not good enough. I still need you to be more specific. You have to tell me what's on the ground there. It's the main part of the entire story. And you've used your second guess. You only get one more."

"You're tough," Mrs. Elliott laughed. "Give me a hint. Is that a coin?"

Grace twisted her mouth and scrunched her eyes, obviously struggling with the idea of giving any more clues.

"Okay," she finally relented, "I'll give you a hint, but I think I've helped too much already. Yes, that is a coin."

"Is it some kind of special coin?"

"Come on, that's two hints," said Grace. "Fine. It's a very special coin."

A strange look came over Mrs. Elliott's face as if remembering something that she would rather forget.

"I give up," she finally replied, forcing a smile. "You win. Tell me about your picture."

Grace was delighted with her victory.

"You were so close," Grace said joyfully. "It's a story about something my sister and her friends have been investigating. Years ago, this little boy found an old Romanian coin on the downtown sidewalk. Wait, or was it a Roman coin? I forget. Anyway, the boy put it into a gumball machine at the pharmacy. Guess what? The coin turned out to be worth a billion dollars. Well, actually, I don't remember how much it was worth, but I know that it was a whole lot. And our friend Chief, who leads our Bible Club, and who used to be the Chief of Police, thought the coin had been stolen. According to him, the owner of the dry cleaners is a fence. Now, just in case you think that I mean a fence around a yard, I don't. I'm just using a fancy term that people who know about stolen things often use."

"Personally, I don't think they should use the word fence like that, do you? Every time they say fence, I think of the white picket fence around my Nana's house. They should call it something different. Anyway, the police could never prove that Mr. Miller was a fence. Sounds funny when I say it like that, doesn't it? Mr. Miller was a fence. You might as well say that Mr. Miller was a house, or Mr. Miller was a driveway."

While Grace spoke, Mrs. Elliott had turned pale.

"What does the girl have to do with it?" she asked timidly.

"Oh," answered Grace, her eyes growing wide, "that's part of the mystery. Apparently, all those years ago, the little boy who found the coin told the police that he had seen this dancing girl on the street that day. I like that part of the story. I've been imagining that the girl is an angel and that she dropped the coin on the sidewalk so the little boy would find it."

"Does anyone know who the dancing girl is?"

"No, but it's too bad. Abigail and her friends said that the girl might be the only way to solve the crime. For according to the police, there were lots of other coins stolen too, and nobody ever found them. But unless they can connect the coin to the fence, there's nothing else anyone can do. That's funny. Did you hear what I said? They need to connect the coin to the fence. Maybe they could just glue it to the fence. Get it? They could *glue* the coin to the *fence* and then it would be *connected*."

But Mrs. Elliott didn't respond.

"Are you okay, Mrs. Elliott? You don't look so good."

"Abigail, Abigail," Grace shouted as she ran into the toddler room, "you've got to come quick."

Abigail looked up. She had been playing dolls with two-year-old Jenny Carmichael.

"What's wrong?" Abigail asked, "Is someone hurt?"

"No, no," Grace answered. "Mrs. Elliott needs to talk to you right away. It's very important."

"I can't go," replied Abigail, "there are still three kids who haven't been picked up by their parents yet."

"That's okay, Abigail," said Mrs. Everhardt, who was also working the toddler room, "I'll finish up. You go ahead."

Just as Abigail began thanking Mrs. Everhardt, Grace shrieked. Timmy Wilson had begun chasing her around the room, and he was making chomping motions with his mouth.

Abigail quickly picked Timmy up, being careful to hold him at arm's length.

"No biting, Timmy," Abigail said as she placed him inside a circular infant gate. "Okay, Grace, let's go."

At eight o'clock the same evening, Declan and Zayne were hanging out in Declan's room.

Sitting at a desk covered in plastic model airplane parts, Declan was working on a meticulous reproduction of the Wright Brothers first airplane, the 1903 Flyer One. And Zayne lay on the floor nearby, reading a book called *Weird and Random Facts*; his now infamous ducky boots removed and strewn conspicuously about the room.

"Did you know the waffle iron was invented in the Middle Ages?" Zayne asked his friend.

"Uh, no," Declan replied absently while trying to glue a propeller to his plane.

"It was originally invented to make communion wafers."

"Oh, that's nice," said Declan, pretending to listen.

"In the late thirteen hundreds," Zayne continued, "the first known waffle recipe was recorded in a letter from a husband to his wife." Zayne looked up. "I guess he liked his waffles a particular way, and he didn't want her to mess them up. I'm like that too. I like them just a bit brown on top with lots of whipped cream."

"Hmm."

Zayne returned to his reading.

"It has been remarked about French King Francois I that he 'les amait beacoup.' That's French for he 'loved them a lot.'"

"Really," Declan muttered as he began working on the second propeller.

Realizing that Declan hadn't been listening, Zayne tried a new approach.

"Wow, how about this!" he began with a grin. "It says here that the first waffles were actually made out of rocks, and when people tried to eat them their teeth would all fall out."

"That's nice."

"Also," Zayne added, trying not to laugh, "in the sixteen hundreds, a man from the Netherlands invented a waffle that would make you fly. That's where the legend of the Flying Dutchman comes from."

"How about that," Declan replied while the redhead bit his lip in an attempt to keep himself from busting up.

Before Zayne could utter any more nonsense, the phone could be heard ringing downstairs.

Someone answered it. Zayne began again.

"And, did you know that waffles are actually a vegetable?"

"Declan," his mom shouted, "the phone is for you. I think it's Abigail."

"Okay, Mom, I'll be right there."

Declan set down his glue bottle and tweezers and got up from his chair. Meanwhile, Zayne could no longer contain himself and had begun rolling on the floor in hysterics.

"What are you laughing about?" Declan asked with a confused look on his face.

"Waffles, Declan. Waffles."

Declan shook his head. "You know that you don't always make a lot of sense, right?" he added as he left the room and headed down the stairs.

When he reached the kitchen, his mom handed him the phone.

"Hello," he said.

"Declan?" Abigail's voice asked.

"Yeah, it's Declan."

"Declan, it's Abigail. The most incredible thing ever has happened. You are NEVER going to believe it."

"What?" wondered Declan, caught off guard. "What's happened?"

"We've found her."

"Found who?"

"We've found the dancing girl."

Chapter Thirteen

"My maiden name is Miller," revealed Mrs. Elliott to the Bible Club, who were crowded into the living room of her tiny home. "And yes, my father is Frank Miller, the owner of the dry cleaners."

"Blimey! So it was you who Alex Townsend saw on the day he found the coin," declared Talia in amazement.

"Yes, it was."

"And you are the one who put the coin on the sidewalk?" asked Tomas.

"Yes."

"But why?" wondered Miles.

After taking a sip from a glass of tea, Mrs. Elliott shifted nervously in her chair.

"Because I knew the coin had been stolen," she answered simply.

The investigators listened intently as she resumed.

"I was fourteen-years-old, and I had come to realize that my Dad was a crook." She paused to take another sip, and several members of the Bible Club noticed that her hands trembled slightly. "For as long as I could remember, Dad had always had his backdoor customers, as I had begun to call them, showing up at the dry cleaners. They came in from the alley behind the store, and whenever they arrived, Dad would quickly shew me out the front. Not that I visited him there all that much. Sadly, the truth is that my dad was, and still is, an angry man who never really wanted me around. But sometimes, if my mom had to run an errand or something, I would get dropped off at the shop."

"As far back as I can remember, I suspected that my dad did more than just clean people's clothes, but I didn't know exactly what. Finally, I put all the pieces together. For starters, the backdoor customers were not a very respectable group of people. They looked dishonest, if you know what I mean, and it didn't take much for me to begin imagining that they might be criminals. Then there was the money. My dad ran a tiny dry cleaning business, so how did he afford the amazing vacations we took each summer? Or the brand new car every couple years? Or, and this became a major clue, his rare coin collection?"

This comment sent a gigantic wave of excitement through the Bible Club.

"Supposedly, coins were his hobby," Mrs. Elliott continued with a frown. "And whenever he got new ones, he loved to show them off to me. In fact, it seemed to be the only time he ever wanted me around. But I began to get a funny feeling, wondering if he wanted to show me the coins simply because he couldn't show them to anyone else. Soon I'd have my answer."

Once again, she returned to her tea. And after a final swallow, she carefully placed the now empty cup onto a coffee table.

"One day, I needed something or other for school, and my mom wasn't home. So, I stopped by Dad's shop. But a funny thing happened, the front door was locked. Now, my Dad only loves two things, money and work, and so for the store to be closed during normal business hours seemed very odd. Curious, I went around to the back door. But as soon as I entered the alley, I stopped. I could hear voices talking, and one of them was Dad. You see, there's a tiny window on that side of the shop which my dad only opens when it's really hot. Well, it was really hot that day, and he must not have realized that he still had the window open because you could hear the entire conversation."

Abigail, who was taking notes with her pink pen, scribbled frantically as she tried to record every detail.

"He was talking to another man, and the other man was very angry. He said that Dad had promised him that he could sell the coins fast but that it had been over three months. My dad sounded angry too, yet also a little bit scared. He said that he never promised that he could sell the coins that fast. The theft had been in all the papers, he added, and his usual clients were leery of buying until things died down. He said that if he pushed too hard it would lead the police to him. And if the police found him, my dad said, it would lead to everyone getting caught. This caused the other man to back down a bit. The angry man told Dad that he could have a little bit more time but that he needed to get the coins sold. Frightened that they might be coming out into the alley, I ran away as fast as I could."

"Did you tell anyone?" asked Miles.

"I told my mom, but I think she already knew. She just said that I must have misunderstood. Yet, what was there to misunderstand?"

"What did you do next?" wondered Talia.

"Unfortunately, I didn't do anything. He isn't the nicest person, but he's still my dad, and I was afraid of getting him into trouble. Not to mention, I was also afraid of what would happen to me if he found out that I snitched on him."

Sensing the need to change the direction of the conversation, Declan asked Mrs. Elliott to tell them about the Roman coin.

"Over the course of the next year, the backdoor customers continued to come and go. Then one day, while in the store, my dad showed me the Roman coin that he'd just 'gotten.' He was ecstatic. All he kept saying was that it was worth a fortune. But I knew what he really meant; he could make a fortune selling it. Yet, something unexpected happened. While he still had the coin out, a dry cleaning customer came in. We were in the back, and no one could see us, but Dad panicked. He grabbed the coin and, at the same time, pushed a button underneath his desk. Amazingly, a secret drawer opened on the desk's back side. My dad quickly dropped the coin in the drawer, pressed it closed, and ran off to attend to the customer, leaving me alone in the room."

"I have no idea what possessed me to do it. It was my conscience, I guess. Or, maybe it was the Holy Spirit, although I hadn't become a Christian yet. But however you explain it, as I heard Dad talking with the customer, I just went for it. I pushed the button, grabbed the coin from the secret drawer, closed the drawer again, and left out the back of the store. Like I said, I hadn't thought it through, so I had no idea what I was going to do next. My first thought was to take the coin to the police. However, I couldn't do it. Dad might go to prison and it would be my fault. Instead, I just went home and locked myself in my room. Yet soon, a crazy plan came to me. I wouldn't give the coin to the police. I would let someone else do it."

"If I left the coin somewhere out in the open then somebody would find it. Naively, I expected that they would then give it to the police. The only hard part was where to leave it. I finally decided that I would put it outside of Dad's store. I couldn't turn him in, but maybe the police would make the connection. It would be doing the right thing without having to do it myself. At least, that's what I told myself."

"Later that night, I went to put my plan into action. But once I was out in front of the dry cleaners, I began to have second thoughts. I felt scared of him being caught and what that might mean for Mom and me. That must have been when the little boy saw me. I wasn't dancing on the sidewalk." Mrs. Elliott offered a half-smile. "I was pacing back and forth, trying to get up the courage to drop the coin. Finally, I did it. I left the coin and I ran home."

"But things didn't go according to plan," Zayne offered succinctly.

"No, they didn't," Mrs. Elliott agreed. "It was a foolish plan to begin with. Any number of things could have gone wrong. However, I never would have imagined that a little boy would find the coin and stick it in a gumball machine."

"Well," Miles said, "it did wind up getting to the police."

"It did," acknowledged Mrs. Elliott, "but it wasn't found in front of Dad's store. Maybe if it had been he would have gotten caught."

"Did he ever suspect that you had taken the coin?" wondered Declan.

"Amazingly, he didn't. But he was sure mad...scary mad. For weeks, he would storm around our house, yelling that he'd been robbed. I found that to be a bit ironic considering that he and his backdoor customers were the real thieves."

"So did he stop selling the illegal coins after that?" asked Abigail, pausing briefly from her note taking.

"I think so, at first, but it didn't last. Soon he was back at it. That is, until he realized the police were on to him. He stopped then. At least, I think he did, for I never saw the backdoor customers again after that. However, there were several times when money would get tight for us and then, magically, it wouldn't be tight anymore."

"Wow!" exclaimed Tomas, "that's an amazing story. But what do we do now? Can we tell the police?"

"We can't," answered Declan. "Or, I guess I should say that it won't do us any good. I've already talked with Chief. He said the statute of limitations has expired."

"The statute of what?" replied Tomas.

Declan started to reply, but Zayne interrupted him.

"The statute of limitations means that the crime can no longer be prosecuted."

"So he got away with selling all of those stolen coins?" asked Grant.

"He did," Declan confirmed.

"Well," began Talia, "that brings us back to Tomas' question. What do we do now?"

Declan got up and walked over to the window. He silently stared outside for a few moments before speaking.

"In one sense," he began without turning around, "we solved the mystery. We wanted to know how the coin got on the street and if a crime had been committed. Now we know the answer to both of those questions."

"But *now* there are new questions," countered Abigail.

"Yes, that's true," continued Declan as he turned to face his friends. "I see two new questions. The first is, 'Who stole the coin and gave it to Mr. Miller to sell?' And the second is…"

Yet Declan didn't get to finish.

"And the second is," Miles interrupted, "'Where are the rest of the stolen coins?'"

"Exactly," Declan nodded.

Talia pulled her hand through her long black hair. "But how can we answer those questions," she wondered, "unless we…." She purposely left her sentence unfinished.

The entire Bible Club knew what Talia had intended to say, and yet for some time, no one spoke.

Finally, Abigail looked at Mrs. Elliott.

"I know this is a long shot," Abigail said mildly, "but do you think your father would talk with us? Obviously, he knows the answer to the first question, and he might be our only hope of ever answering the second."

Mrs. Elliott thought for a moment and then sighed.

"It would mean that I would have to tell him about dropping the coin on the sidewalk," she replied hesitantly, "but I'll do it. I've been keeping it a secret for too long. However, I can't promise you that he'll admit to anything or that he'll help. And remember, he isn't the nicest man in the world. He might bark at you. Still, if you understand what you are getting in to, it's worth a try. But, he'll *never* speak to a crowd. Pick two people to go with me, and we'll try and visit him this afternoon. Sooner is better than latter or else my courage might fail."

"Splendid," Talia exclaimed. Then she paused and looked around the room. "This is a pretty delicate situation," she added, "I don't think we should just draw straws or play rock-paper-scissors to decide who goes. We need to send our most careful and diplomatic investigators. We need people with great tack; who won't say the wrong thing."

"Fine, fine," Zayne declared, rising from his seat, "you don't have to beat around the bush…"

"No, Zayne," Talia replied, "I don't mean to hurt your feelings. It's just that you don't always…"

But Zayne wasn't listening to her.

"I'd be happy to go," Zayne continued, "but who should go with me? I'm not sure anyone else is as good at being tactful as I am."

There was an awkward silence. Finally, Zayne burst out laughing.

"I'm just kidding," he said after regaining his composure. "I think Abigail and Declan should go."

Several voices echoed their agreement. And so it was decided. Later that afternoon, Abigail and Declan would join Mrs. Elliott in an interview of her father. Yet the Bible Club tried to keep their hopes low, for all of them understood the long odds. Frank Miller wasn't likely to tell them anything.

At a quarter past two, Abigail and Declan met Mrs. Elliott outside of her father's dry cleaning business.

No one, including Mrs. Elliott, was doing a very good job of hiding their nerves. However, Mrs. Elliott began by telling the two investigators how she would start the conversation. First, she would introduce them. Then, she would admit to her father that she was the one that took the Roman coin all those years ago.

"I don't know how he's going to react," Mrs. Elliott told them. "But, if he doesn't lose his temper, maybe you'll be able to ask him a few questions."

An old-fashioned shopkeeper's bell rang as they opened the door and entered. Her father wasn't at the counter, however he soon appeared through a doorway to the back. When he saw his daughter and the children, Mr. Miller didn't bother to come out, nor did he great them. Instead, he disappeared back from where he came. Tentatively, Mrs. Elliott and her two guests made their way to the counter. When Mr. Miller failed to reappear, Mrs. Elliott called to him.

"Dad," she exclaimed, "can I talk to you for a minute?"

"Can't talk," came a stiff reply, "I've got work to do."

"It's important, Dad. It will only take a few minutes."

"Then come back here," was the gruff answer.

So, Mrs. Elliott lifted up a hinged portion of the counter which allowed the three of them to pass. Next, they cautiously walked through the doorway that led them to Mr. Miller. There they saw a thin white-haired man with his back turned. He was pressing shirts on some kind of steam machine. Behind him, a large box, much like a home washer but far bigger, rumbled away noisily.

"Dad," Mrs. Elliott said, "I've got something I need to tell you. But first, these are two friends of mine. This is Abigail and this is Declan."

Mr. Miller grunted in reply but didn't look up from his work.

There was a moment of silence as Mrs. Elliott appeared to be working up her courage. After taking a long deep breath, she began.

"Dad, *I* took the Roman coin from your desk," she blurted.

The old man stopped his work but did not turn around.

"I knew you were selling stolen coins," she continued. "And I wanted you to stop." Having finally revealed her secret, Mrs. Elliott's voice grew stronger. "It was wrong. They didn't belong to you. And yes, I wanted you to get caught, but not because I hated you…but because I loved you. And, I thought that if you got caught maybe you would change. Perhaps it would humble you, and you would let go of all your anger. It's still what I want for you because I still love you."

During Mrs. Elliott's entire speech, her father had still not faced them. However, as she spoke, his body began to tremble. When Mr. Miller began to slowly turn, Mrs. Elliott and the children prepared for a volcano of fury. Instinctively, they all took a step backwards toward the door. Yet when the old man stood looking at them, it wasn't anger that caused him to shake but rather something else…something like remorse.

For a full minute, Mr. Miller stood in silence, staring at his daughter. Finally, he spoke.

"All this time, you knew? You knew that I was a thief. How could you love me? How could you love a thief? I've been...I've been...a terrible father."

"Dad, it hasn't been easy, but I do love you. I've always loved you."

The old man dropped into a chair. He would have cried, but it had been so long that he didn't remember how. Twice it appeared that he began to say "I'm sorry" yet he couldn't spit out the words.

Finally, in the kindest tone he could find, which still sounded like an insult, Mr. Miller pointed to Abigail and Declan and asked, "Who are they?"

It was Declan who replied.

"Sir, my friends and I have been investigating the case of the Roman coin," he said with a courage and authority far beyond his years, "and the trail ends here with you. We know it was twenty years ago, but it appears as if justice has never been done. The coin that your daughter dropped on the sidewalk was just one of many coins that were stolen from a bank in Reynosa, Mexico. Those coins have never been found, and we would like to see them returned to their rightful owner. As for your part in the crime, it can no longer be prosecuted. You have nothing to fear. So, if you can, will you help us? Can you tell us who stole the coins? And do you know where the other coins are?"

Mr. Miller appeared taken aback by the honesty and the boldness of the young man. Yet to the surprise of everyone, he answered Declan's questions directly.

"It was Jaden DeSoto," he said, seeming almost relieved to speak the words. "He was a small time crook from town here. He was into low end jobs, robbing convenience stores and breaking into cars, that kind of stuff. I knew who he was, but he definitely wasn't on the level of the people I'd been working with. Then, apparently, he started thinking he could make it as a coin thief. So he pulled off a few robberies, small ones at first, and then he came to me with the coins. He was clumsy, but he'd actually gotten some pretty good stuff, and I sold it for him. That's what I did, you see, selling stolen coins to big time collectors. Anyway, DeSoto wound up getting caught just like I figured he would, and the judge sent him up state for a few years."

"But one day, about three years later, he shows up here with these priceless Roman coins. He said that a friend of a friend had tipped him off to a huge collection being kept in a tired old bank in Mexico. Ripped them off easy, he said. Now he wanted me to sell the coins. Well, my take on the sale would have gotten me a quarter of a million, so I agreed. I started with just the one coin; he kept the rest. Yet when that boy stole it, I mean found it, and put it into the gumball machine, everything was ruined. Things got too hot to sell, and when I thought things had finally cooled off, I found out that the cops were on to me. So I never sold any of DeSoto's coins. In fact, from what I heard, he couldn't get any of them sold."

"Soon he needed cash and got nabbed knocking over some liquor store. He used a gun too. Between the gun and his prior conviction, they gave him twenty five years. Funny, DeSoto had a couple million in coins but went to jail for a hundred dollar hold up. As far as I know, no one ever found the coins. DeSoto had them stashed, I guess, hoping he could sell them when he got out."

"Has he gotten out?" Abigail asked.

"Yeah, he got out, but not the way he wanted to. Got real sick in prison, from what I heard. Died about a year ago."

"So no one knows where the rest of the coins are?" Declan inquired.

"Nope."

"Well, thank you, Mr. Miller," Declan said. "We really appreciate your help."

As Declan and Abigail were about to go, Mr. Miller gave them a bit of advice.

"Try DeSoto's mom. She lives here in town. If anyone has a clue where the coins are, it could be her." He paused. Then he added with a somewhat knowing tone, "But watch out! When there's millions at stake, there's always some two-bit crook on the prowl."

"Thanks Mr. Miller," smiled Abigail. "We'll be careful."

As Abigail and Declan left the dry cleaners, Mrs. Elliott remained behind to talk more with her father.

"Can you believe that?" Abigail asked Declan while they began to walk home.

However, Declan didn't answer her question. Instead, he whispered, "Look behind you, but don't make it obvious."

Abigail peered over her shoulder.

"What do you see?"

"Nothing," Abigail replied quietly, "just a bald guy with a beard sitting on that bench."

"What's he doing?"

"Nothing."

"Doesn't that seem strange to you?" asked Declan.

"Why would a guy sitting on a bench doing nothing seem strange to me?"

"Because I saw that same guy standing in the alley beside the dry cleaners when we went in."

"So?"

"That was a half hour ago and he's still there. Now he's sitting on a bench directly across from Mr. Miller's shop...still doing nothing. I glanced at him when we left the shop and he tried to pretend that he wasn't watching us."

"Come on," cried Abigail, "what are you saying?"

"I'm saying that when there's millions at stake..." Declan didn't finish his sentence, but Abigail got the point.

Chapter Fourteen

Talia sat at the kitchen table eating a bowl of cereal. Beside her, a Bible lay open to the book of Galatians.

"So in Christ Jesus you are all children of God through faith," Talia read as she crunched on her Raisin Bran, "for all of you who were baptized into Christ have clothed yourselves with Christ. There is neither Jew nor Gentile, neither slave nor free, nor is there male and female, for you are all one in Christ Jesus." She read the last phrase again, "you are all one in Christ Jesus." The words brought a smile to her face.

Although she had never lived in India, Talia still understood the impact of these words. Her skin was dark, and in the land of her parents that would have noteworthy consequences. In India, people had been classified by a caste system for hundreds of years. And the system told you what you could and couldn't do and who you could and couldn't be. Skin color played a large part. Light skin was good and beautiful; dark skin was bad and ugly. And even though she had grown up in Great Britain, the idea had been so ingrained in the Indian community that Talia got the message. But, in Christ, everyone was on equal ground, for grace made sure of that.

Yet the words of Galatians chapter three warmed Talia's heart for another reason—in Christ there was community.

Before coming to the United States, Talia had trouble finding quality friendships. Her father was a highly regarded engineer who led projects around the world. That meant, that like Grant, Talia's family needed to move a lot. But, unlike Grant, Talia was more outgoing and actively sought out new relationships. However, no matter how hard she tried, Talia never felt like she had real community. Until she met Abigail, who invited her to the Bible Club.

And now, for the first time in her life, she had found the kind of friends that she had always longed for.

As Talia finished her breakfast, it was those friends that she couldn't wait to see.

The details of Abigail and Declan's amazing interview with Mr. Miller had already passed from one member of the Bible Club to another. And, later that morning, everyone had agreed to meet at Northside Park. Their plan was to visit Eleanor DeSoto, the mother of the coin thief. For, as Tomas had discovered, Mrs. DeSoto lived just a few blocks from Northside.

While Talia swallowed what remained of her glass of orange juice, she could hear her mother arriving home from her long shift at the hospital.

Talia's mother, Leylani, worked as an emergency room nurse and often worked overnight. When she greeted Talia, Leylani looked tired. But instead of giving Talia a quick kiss and then disappearing up to her bed, as she often did after the late night shift, Leylani sat down beside her daughter at the kitchen table.

Talia expected small talk from her mother, but Leylani had something very different in mind.

"Lia," her mother said excitedly, "I must tell you something."

"Sure, Mum, what is it?"

"It's about that man you just told me about, Frank Miller. He was admitted into the emergency room last night."

"He was?" Talia replied in surprise. "What happened?"

"About eight-thirty, the ambulance brought him in, and I was assigned to his care. He had a broken arm and bruises all over his face."

"Are you kidding?"

"No, I'm not kidding," Talia's mother answered. "It looked like someone beat him up pretty bad."

Talia gasped.

"In situations like that, it's the hospital's normal procedure to call in the police," Leylani continued, "but he wouldn't speak to them."

"Not at all?"

"Not at all. He completely refused. Lia, I don't like you getting mixed up in this."

"Mum," Talia said, trying to hide her nervous excitement, "I'll be fine. But I've got to go. I've got to tell the others what happened."

"Okay," replied her mother, "but be careful!"

However, Talia didn't hear her, for she was already out the door.

"Zayne," Abigail said with disdain, "why are you *still* wearing those frog boots?"

"Three reasons," replied Zayne as he stood near the edge of the lake at Northside Park. "The first is that they are extremely comfortable. The second is that I really like frogs. And the third is that they are very practical."

"Frog boots are practical?" questioned Abigail.

"Yes," answered Zayne while taking several steps into the lake. "See, because of my boots I can go places that you simply can't."

"So if someone told you to go jump in a lake you would be able to do it," added Declan with a smile.

"Without getting wet," grinned Zayne.

But as Zayne tried to walk back onto the shore, something went wrong. He couldn't move.

"Help!" he cried.

"What's the matter?" asked Miles.

"I appear to have sunken into the bank's soft mud, and I'm stuck. The suction is too strong."

After watching Zayne struggle for some time, Grant came to his rescue.

Approaching the edge of the bank, Grant reached out, put both of his arms beneath Zayne's, and easily lifted his friend from the water. Unfortunately, the froggy boots remained behind, still stuck in the mud. The others made a poor attempt to hide their amusement as Zayne frantically attempted to retrieve his boots.

Over and over again, he would stretch from the bank, get his fingertips on the boots, and pull. But they wouldn't budge.

As Zayne continued his struggle, Tomas arrived. Then, shortly afterward, a somewhat frantic Talia appeared.

With the entire Bible Club now present, Talia explained that she had incredible news.

"Well, tell us," exclaimed Abigail, knowing that it must be something important to rile up the normally subdued Talia.

"Okay," Talia began, "but you aren't going to believe this. My mom was working the overnight shift at the…"

Yet Talia didn't get to finish her sentence, for at that moment a loud splash stole everyone's attention. It was, of course, Zayne. Having reached too far in his last attempt to retrieve his boots, he had slipped and fallen face-first into the lake.

A few seconds later, he emerged from the water holding a froggy boot in each hand. He was soaking wet.

Laughter ensued, and lasted several minutes, before Abigail finally managed to ask if he was okay.

Zayne responded that he was fine. However, when he flipped his boots over and a stream of water poured out, the laughter erupted once more.

When everyone had finally calmed down again, the Bible Club felt genuine compassion for their drenched friend. Unable to do anything for him, and since he didn't want to go home, they all gathered around a picnic table and turned their attention back to Talia.

But as they listened to her news any lingering smiles soon faded.

"Someone beat up Mr. Miller," Tomas said with a look of shock.

"Why?" asked Miles.

"I don't know," answered Talia, "but remember the warning he gave us, 'When there's millions at stake, there's always some two-bit crook on the prowl.'"

"Yeah," exclaimed Declan, "and remember the guy I told you about? I'm sure he was watching Mr. Miller's shop. What if he turned out to be the guy who beat him up?"

"That's scary," Abigail replied, her face turning pale.

"That is scary," seconded Talia. "But what I don't understand is why Mr. Miller didn't talk to the police."

Zayne, who stood dripping at the head of the picnic table, offered a theory. "I imagine he didn't talk to the police because he didn't want it to lead to questions about his past."

Declan nodded his agreement.

"Well, what do we do now?" Abigail asked slowly, looking at her friends one by one. "This has certainly taken a more serious tone."

"Yes, it has," acknowledged Miles, "but I don't think it changes our next move. We're here to see if Jaden DeSoto's mom has any ideas about the location of the stolen coins. And, danger or no danger, I think that's what we've got to do." The anxious expressions of his friends revealed that not everyone was so sure. So he continued, "Yes, we're kids, but what does that matter? Right is still right and wrong is still wrong. Remember that verse we talked about last month from the book of James, 'anyone then who knows the good they ought to do but doesn't do it, sins.' Well, I know the good we ought to do, so let's do it."

"I understand what you're saying, Miles," replied Abigail, "but turning this over to the police might be the better thing to do."

"Do you think they'll believe us?" offered Tomas. "And even if they do, do you think they'll follow up on this like we will, and in the time frame that we can?"

"And if they don't," suggested Declan, "it might be too late. For if someone really is out there looking for the coins, there's no time to lose."

A silence followed as the friends thought through everything that had been said. Finally, Grant spoke up.

"We've come this far," he said, "and danger or no danger, we need to see this to the end. Remember, we've got Chief. If we keep going and we run into any trouble, he'll be there to help us. Don't let fear win."

Grant's words were both unexpected and powerful, and the argument was settled.

But while everyone agreed that danger wouldn't stop the investigation, they also agreed that the wise thing would be to keep Chief in the loop. And if he felt it necessary for them to turn things over to the police, they would.

So with the investigation to continue, the Bible Club began the short walk to the home of Mrs. Irene DeSoto.

With no one wanting to be left out, the friends decided they would all just go to Mrs. DeSoto's front door, hoping the large group didn't overwhelm their interviewee. Everyone would go, that is, except Zayne, who they left across the street drip-drying in the morning sun.

After Declan knocked, a frail elderly woman promptly answered the door.

"Excuse me," Abigail asked kindly, "are you Mrs. Irene DeSoto?"

"Yes, children, come in, come in," she insisted as if she had been expecting them. "I'm so glad you are here. Follow me." Unsure what to say, the Bible Club followed her down a short hallway and then into a rather unattractive green and red living room. When they had arrived, Mrs. DeSoto turned to them and spoke once more. "I'm glad the church sent so many of you, for the furniture is very heavy." Pointing vaguely at the north end of the room, she continued, "You can have the bookshelves, and the books too, the arm chair, the ottoman, and the love seat. I'm not sure how much they are worth, but hopefully they will bring you something at the rummage sale."

When Mrs. DeSoto had finished, Talia gave her a gentle smile and then politely corrected her. "I'm sorry, Mrs. DeSoto," she said. "There seems to be some kind of mistake. You see, we aren't here about the rummage sale."

"You're not?" the woman puzzled. "Aren't you from the church?"

"Well, sort of," Talia replied with a shy giggle. "You see, we are a Bible study group, we call ourselves the Bible Club, but we aren't here about the rummage sale. Actually, we kind of got ourselves wrapped up in a titchy…"

"She means tiny," Abigail corrected.

"Yes, sorry," Talia continued, "we got ourselves wrapped up in a tiny mystery, and that's why we're here."

"A mystery," Mrs. DeSoto said, looking quite confused. "I'm not sure how I could help you with a mystery. The Good Lord knows that I'm not the best educated woman around. I spent fifty years housekeeping at the Lawson Hotel, I did. Dropped out of school when I was fourteen to take the job. I had to help out my parents. Money was tight. Anyway, unless the mystery was about folding sheets or doing laundry, I'm afraid I'd be no good to you. I can't even solve the Sunday crossword puzzle, so what makes you think an old woman like me could help you?"

"It's a mystery that involves your son, Jaden," Talia added delicately.

"Imagine that," replied the little old lady, "all these years and no one ever wants to talk about Jaden, God rest his soul. He made some mistakes, that's for sure, and got sent to prison for them. But if I even mention his name everybody just gives me the cold shoulder. I guess that's what happens when your only son becomes a criminal. Strange though, I never get visitors. Then suddenly, everyone wants to visit, and they want to talk about Jaden too! How strange…how very strange."

"Someone else was here asking about Jaden?" Abigail asked.

"Yes, the man from the church came by yesterday. He said they were having a rummage sale and asked if there was anything I could donate. The money would help some orphans, he said. But once I invited him in, all he wanted to talk about was Jaden."

"What did the man look like?" questioned Abigail.

"He was a young man. But, of course, when you are my age, everyone seems young. He was bald on top but had a thick beard. To tell you the truth, he didn't seem like he was from a church. It wasn't his appearance, for grace is for all of us, no matter what we look like. No, it was his personality. His friendliness seemed a bit…phony. To me, cold and harsh seemed more his true nature, and those certainly aren't fruits of the Spirit. Yet I'm a sinner too, so if he says he's a Christian, who am I to judge?"

"That sounds exactly like the man outside the dry cleaners," Declan whispered to the others.

"What did he want?" continued Talia.

"Like I said," Mrs. DeSoto answered, "he told me that he wanted items for a rummage sale. Although, when I offered the books and things, he acted like he didn't really want them at all. He said that he would send someone by to pick them up, but it sounded like a story to me. However, when you all showed up on my doorstep, I thought, 'my goodness, he really has sent someone.' But now it appears that it was just a story after all."

"I'm sorry if he lied to you," Talia said politely. "What did he want to know about your son?"

"Funny that. He said that he had met Jaden. Although, how they'd met he wouldn't say, even though I asked him several times. Anyway, he wanted to know if Jaden had sent me anything from prison, a letter or anything. Come to think of it, he also never explained how he knew that Jaden was in prison. Well, I told him that Jaden never wrote. He had nice handwriting, always had, ever since elementary school. But he never wrote letters. He would call me every so often, that is, when he was allowed. But no, Jaden didn't write. Then the man asked if I had been sent Jaden's personal items, you know, after he died. To which I answered that I hadn't been sent anything at all. Now come to think of it, how did he know that Jaden had died? Before leaving, he asked if he could take a look at Jaden's old room. However, I told him there was nothing to see. Jaden moved out at eighteen and took everything he owned with him. Where the stuff is now, God only knows."

"I see," Talia replied.

"So children, that's enough about rummage sales and strangers. What is it you wanted to know?"

"You seem to have told us everything already," Abigail stated. "The truth is, we think your son may have hidden some valuable coins somewhere, and we wondered if he might have told you where. Or perhaps that he might have sent you something which could locate the coins. But it doesn't sound like that happened."

Mrs. DeSoto shook her head.

"I'm sorry. I don't know anything about hidden coins, and I sure don't have a treasure map. I wish the other fellow would have just told the truth instead of playing all of his pretend games."

"We are sorry to have bothered you, Mrs. DeSoto," offered Talia. "God bless you."

"You weren't any bother at all. It's nice to have some company for a change. And it's nice to talk about Jaden. God bless you all too."

The friends made their way back down the hall to the front door. As they were saying their final goodbyes, Declan suddenly stopped. Then, he turned back toward Mrs. DeSoto with a curious expression on his face.

"Mrs. DeSoto," he began, "I know you said that Jaden never wrote, but did he ever send you a Mother's Day card or a birthday card?"

"Why sure. Mother's Day, my birthday, and Christmas. Even when he got sick with the cancer he still always sent me cards. I think the last one arrived just a few weeks before he died."

"Do you still have it?" Declan asked excitedly.

"Yes."

"Would you mind if we look at it?"

"Not at all."

Mrs. DeSoto disappeared down the hall and around a corner.

Soon she returned with a plain white envelope upon which 'To Mother' had been written in a neat cursive style on the front. She handed it to Declan, who opened it carefully. On the cover of the card read your standard Mother's Day fare, but as he turned to the inside, a thin piece of paper slid into his hand. Declan's eyes grew wide. Inside the card itself, beneath the typical sappy message, there was a note signed by Jaden. Declan read it out loud.

Mom,

I hope you have a happy Mother's Day. I'm sorry I didn't turn out to be a very good son. But I'm going to make it up to you. I've been really sick with this cancer. The doctor says it's in my brain now. It's been making it hard to remember things. But I can tell that I'm getting better. I've only got two years left on my sentence, and when I get out, the first thing I'm going to do is come and visit you. I've got some money stashed away, and I'm going to use it to help make things easier for you. I've been going to the church service here every week. The pastor has been talking to me too. And I've been reading my Bible. You'd be so proud of me. I'm a real

163

Christian now, Mom, like you. My favorite verse is Matthew 6:21, "Where your treasure is, there your heart will be also." I like that. My heart's in the right place now, Ma. I'm going to take care of you.

Love,

Jaden

P.S. Hold on to the piece of paper in the card. It has a few numbers I'll need when I get home. I thought I'd better send them to you, just in case I couldn't remember.

Then, Declan turned his attention to the small piece of loose leaf paper that had fallen from the card. It contained the following list of numbers:

19 2 6 23 6 6 19 60 7 26 42 17 40 7 13 26 42 16 1 35 8

"He called me about a month before," said Mrs. DeSoto as she wiped a tear from her eye, "saying all the same stuff. He'd repeat himself though, forgetting what he already had said. It was the cancer, I suppose. But this card…it was the last time…" Mrs. DeSoto didn't finish. After a brief pause, she looked directly at Grant.

"I'm glad he gave his life to Jesus," she said, "aren't you?"

"Yes," Grant replied, quickly breaking eye contact.

"This list," began Declan, "could we…?"

Mrs. DeSoto interrupted him. "You can take the paper if you think it might help you. I don't have any use for it. Those numbers don't mean anything to me."

A few moments later, the friends were outside Mrs. DeSoto's, walking down her sidewalk toward the street.

"Amazing," Miles declared. "Absolutely amazing. It sure sounded like Jaden DeSoto was coming home for some hidden coins, didn't it?"

"It sure did," seconded Abigail. "And how about that list? It has to be a clue; it just has to be. Where's the paper? Can I see it again?"

The investigators stared at one another. "Who's got the list?" asked Declan. "And where's Tomas?"

A second later, Tomas scampered out the front door and down the steps of Mrs. DeSoto's house. In one hand was the precious paper.

"Sorry, I was just…" Tomas began. However, he didn't get to complete his thought for a whirlwind followed.

As soon as Tomas had stepped from the porch to the sidewalk, a man leapt from behind the bushes. With his left hand, the stranger snatched the paper from Tomas, grabbing it away so forcefully that he knocked the boy upon the ground. Then, in an instant, the man pushed his way through the Bible Club and dashed down the sidewalk to the street. He began to turn to his right, but Zayne suddenly appeared.

Having jumped out from behind a bush of his own, the redhead was now barefoot, and he was holding something in front of him.

Zayne didn't try to stop the man. Instead, he stood directly in the man's path.

The stranger was briefly startled, but after quickly regaining his composure, the man changed his course and ran away in the other direction.

As the excitement came to a close, the friends quickly gathered around Tomas to make sure that he was alright. Other than a scrapped knee, he seemed unharmed.

"Who was that?" asked a frightened Abigail.

"Don't you remember?" answered Declan, staring off in the direction of the perpetrator, "that was the man sitting outside of Mr. Miller's." He paused for a moment and then added, "And my guess is that he's the same man who visited Mrs. DeSoto yesterday."

"Oh my," cried Talia, "and now he's got the only clue to the location of the stolen coins!"

Chapter Fifteen

"*Now* do we get the police?" asked Abigail.

"And tell them what," answered Miles, "that someone stole a piece of paper out of our hands?"

"There's more to it than that," declared Talia, coming to Abigail's defense. "He roughed up Mr. Miller and lied to Mrs. DeSoto."

"That's probably true," Declan agreed, "but we can't prove it."

"Well, what else can we do?" Abigail wondered as she and her friends began to slowly walk toward the park. "This is no longer an investigation, it's a treasure hunt. And the only copy of our possible treasure map is in the hands of the bad guy."

"No," said Tomas with a huge smile, "that wasn't the only copy."

Everyone stopped and stared at Tomas.

"What do you mean?" Talia asked, expressing the question that was in everyone's mind.

"That's why I had fallen behind," Tomas replied as he removed his backpack and pulled out the Case File. "I was logging the numbers into evidence."

"You mean you made a copy of the list!" exclaimed Declan.

"Yes, that's exactly what I mean."

Everyone let out a loud cheer as they hugged and high-fived their friend.

"I have the numbers," Tomas said with a shrug, "but I don't understand them."

"We'll figure that out," Abigail responded. "But first, there are a couple of other things that need some clarification. For instance," she turned to look at Zayne, "what were you doing back there, jumping out from behind that bush like you did? And where are your boots?"

"Oh yeah," Zayne declared, "I almost forgot. Does anyone have five dollars I can borrow? She won't let me have my boots back unless I come up with five dollars."

"I've got five dollars," began Miles, "and you don't have to borrow it; you can have it. But what are you talking about? Who won't let you have your boots back?

"The woman at the corner drug store over there," Zayne said as he pointed to a small shop about two blocks away. "The camera cost five dollars and I didn't have any money, but I had to have it. So I begged the woman at the counter, and she said that I could take it on two conditions. First, I had to promise that I would come back later to pay for it. Second, I had to leave something valuable as collateral. All I had was my froggy boots, however I assured her that they were worth far more than five dollars."

"I know that I say this to you far too often," Abigail stated with her head tilted sideways and a confused look on her face, "but what are you talking about?"

"Oh, yes, well," stammered Zayne, "I guess I should start at the beginning. As you remember, because of that unfortunate accident with the lake this morning, I couldn't join you all in your interview of Mrs. DeSoto. Thus, I was standing across the street in a patch of warm sunlight, allowing the sun's heat to dry my clothes. However, as I waited, I eyed someone suspicious lurking in the bushes beside Mrs. DeSoto's house. And although I couldn't get a clear look at him, it appeared that he might fit the description that Declan had given regarding the man outside the dry cleaners."

"I wasn't quite sure what to do. At first I thought I would try to scare him off, but that didn't seem like a very safe idea. Then I thought I would knock on the door and come join you. At least then I could warn everyone. However, something better occurred to me. It was a long shot, but if I could get his picture, we might be able to find out who he was. Now, I'd seen that small pharmacy on our way up from the park, and I wondered if I might be able to get a camera there. So I raced over as fast as I could. All they had was this," Zayne said, holding out the small rectangular box that he had been carrying in his right hand. "It's one of those disposable cameras that people used to use. You know, the ones where you would turn the entire camera in and then have the film developed."

His friends looked at him blankly, for they had never heard of disposable cameras.

"Anyway," Zayne continued, "I left my boots as collateral and raced back to Mrs. DeSoto's. I had just hidden myself when you guys came out."

"Are you telling us that when you jumped in front of him you took his picture?" Declan asked in amazement.

"I took three pictures actually," Zayne answered. "But the woman at the pharmacy warned me that the camera was pretty old. She wasn't sure if the film would still develop."

"Wow!" Abigail exclaimed. "How incredibly brave."

"And clever," added Talia.

"Now how do we get the pictures?" wondered Grant.

"I bet Chief can do it," replied Declan. "His hobby is photography, and I'm pretty sure he still develops traditional film."

"Then let's get over there," declared Tomas, "and get a closer look at this creep."

"Yeah, and we can start examining Jaden DeSoto's mysterious list of numbers," said Miles.

"Wait," interrupted Abigail, "there's still one more thing I want to know." She turned toward Declan. "In all the excitement, we are forgetting that we almost left Mrs. DeSoto's with nothing, which would have left this entire mystery at a dead end. Declan, what made you ask Mrs. DeSoto about a Mother's Day card?"

"I don't know," Declan replied quietly. "Or, well, I guess I do know, but I don't really understand."

His friends waited for him to explain.

"As we were making our way back down the hallway," he continued, "I realized we were in serious trouble. If visiting Mrs. DeSoto didn't lead us to a clue about the location of the coins, we didn't really have much hope of ever finding them. So as we were walking, I prayed. It wasn't a big prayer or anything, just a simple 'God, what do we do now' kind of thing. And I know it might sound totally crazy, but as soon as I finished, I suddenly thought about the last birthday card my grandparents sent me. Well, it seemed totally random and irrelevant at first, but then I wondered, 'maybe coin thieves send cards too.'"

"Blimey," proclaimed Talia, "do you think it was God?"

"I," Declan hesitated, "I think so, yes."

"Well," began Abigail, "I definitely think it was God. I think He answered your prayer in order to help us with our investigation. Now let's get over to Chief's house and see if he can develop those pictures."

"And see what we can make of this list of numbers," added Miles.

"We can't," Zayne said frantically.

"Why not?" Declan asked.

"Because I don't have my froggy boots back yet."

The Bible Club had spent the entire afternoon at Chief's house, working on the mysterious list of numbers sent to Mrs. DeSoto by her coin-stealing son Jaden. Piles of crumpled papers were strewn around the room, each a failed attempt to decipher the list's meaning.

"I just don't see how we are ever going to figure this out," an exasperated Declan cried as he paced the room holding a clipboard. "The numbers don't seem to substitute for letters in any way I can figure out. And if it is some kind of encrypted code, how are we going to solve it without the key?"

Zayne, who was curled up like a cat in Chief's favorite chair, agreed, "It does seem that our probability of success is nearly zero. There must be a key. It would tell us how the numbers substitute for letters or words. But the key could be anything. It could be a single word. Or, it could be a book, with the list referring to different pages or paragraphs. Who knows?"

"Ugh," exclaimed Miles while throwing another failed attempt onto the floor, "I give up. Grant and I wondered if the numbers might be latitude and longitude, but it creates a treasure map that would take us halfway around the world."

"My brain hurts," Tomas mumbled. He sat across from Miles and Grant at a folding table they had set up in the living room. His head was down, buried in his arms.

Talia was on the floor in front of the couch surrounded by more papers. "Mine too," she echoed as she rubbed her tired eyes.

Just then, Abigail came bursting into the room from the garage.

"He did it," she exclaimed. "He developed them, and we've got something."

Amateur photography had been Chief's hobby for twenty years, and although most of his work was now digital, he still maintained a small dark room in his garage for developing film. While the others had been working to decode the numbers, Chief tried to get the images from Zayne's disposable camera. Abigail had served as his assistant.

"Come on," she continued, "you've got to see this." And she disappeared once more into the garage.

Energized by Abigail's announcement, the others quickly scampered after her.

Once in the garage, everyone crammed themselves as best they could into Chief's small darkroom. The only light in the tiny room came from a single red bulb dangling from the ceiling. Its red glow illuminated an enlarging machine, several pans filled with chemicals, and a clothesline, where four pieces of photographic paper were hanging from clothespins. Just beyond the clothesline stood Chief, his eyes focused intently on one particular paper.

"Chief, did you really do it?" Tomas asked impatiently. "Did you really get the pictures off Zayne's camera?"

"I did," Chief replied, "and you won't believe what we've got." He took a photograph down from the clothesline and handed it to Tomas. "This one's my favorite."

Tomas looked at it carefully and then scowled.

"This…this…looks like a thumb," Tomas proclaimed.

"It is," answered Chief. "Zayne's thumb to be exact. I have another one just like it, but that's my favorite. You can almost make out his fingerprint on that one. It might come in handy someday, if we ever suspect Zayne of committing a crime."

"Oh no," Talia cried. "Do you mean that all we've got is a picture of Zayne's thumb?"

"No," replied Chief, "I've also got a photograph of his pants' pocket. He must have put the camera in there on the way over to my house."

"I did," Zayne confirmed sheepishly. "I'm sorry everybody. I guess I screwed up again."

"Wait, Zayne," Chief interrupted. "There's one more photograph." He removed the picture that he had been staring at and handed it to Zayne. The young red-headed boy literally jumped for joy while a huge smile crossed Chief's face.

"You did it, Zayne," beamed Chief. "You got a perfect picture of our suspect. It couldn't be any clearer."

Everyone cheered, and hugs ensued.

After the picture had been passed around so that everyone could have a look, the friends made their way back to the living room.

"This guy is scary," Abigail said as she handed the photo back to Chief. "Those dark eyes are so threatening."

"That bald head and the thick black beard certainly don't help either," added Talia.

"Or the evil scowl," Tomas continued.

"Or the huge muscles," noted Zayne. "If I had seen him more clearly beforehand, I don't think I would have had the courage to jump out and take his picture."

"How old do you think he is?" Miles wondered.

"His mid-thirties, I'd guess," replied Grant.

"Yes," confirmed Chief as he glanced once more at the photo, "I'd say that's probably right."

Declan moved beside Chief and pointed at the picture.

"So we have our bad guy," he said, "who also apparently believes that there are more coins hidden somewhere. But who is he? And how are we going to beat him to those coins if we don't have the slightest idea what Jaden DeSoto's list of numbers means?"

"That's assuming that they mean anything," interjected Abigail while she twirled her hair around her familiar pink pen. "Remember, he was having trouble with his memory when he wrote that note. Maybe it's just a bunch of nonsense."

"Well," began Chief, waving the photo, "I don't know what to do about that strange list of numbers, but I do know what to do with this picture. I'll send it down to some friends at the station and see if they can help us I.D. this guy. They have a computer that will try to match his facial features with criminals in the F.B.I. database."

"That would be great," said Talia. "At least then we might know who we are up against."

As soon as Talia finished her sentence, everyone grew quite, for they heard the sound of Chief's front door slowly opening and closing.

No one said a word as soft footsteps moved down the hallway. A look of anxiety passed from one member of the Bible Club to another. Even Chief, who had seen more than his fair share of trouble, looked tense.

Out of the corner of his eye, Miles noticed the former policeman tightening his grip around the handle of his cane.

And then, suddenly, someone unexpected burst into the room.

Chapter Sixteen

"Hi guys," said Grace, holding her Bible under her arm. "I'm ready for Bible study. What's wrong with all of you? Did I scare you or something?"

Everyone let out a collective sigh.

"You don't have to be scared of me," Grace continued, "I'm just a seven-year-old girl."

"We thought you might be someone else," her sister replied.

"Well, I'm not," Grace declared as she threw herself down onto the couch. "Are we going to have a study or aren't we? And I hope there's some food. I haven't had my dinner. I came straight over from Katie's house."

"Food, yes," said Chief with a chuckle, "I bet everyone's hungry. It is dinner time. Let me throw some hot dogs and hamburgers on the grill, and then we can have our study. Amidst all the excitement, I almost forgot what night it was."

About an hour later, everyone had eaten their fill, which in Zayne's case included two hamburgers, three hot dogs, and a full-size bag of chips. With their hunger now satisfied, everyone settled into their typical spots for Bible study.

"I know you all have a lot on your minds," Chief began as he gingerly propped his bad knee up on the footrest of his recliner. "But let's put all of that aside for a few minutes and get back to our study on Jesus. Does anyone remember where we left off?"

"I do," said Miles, "we were in Matthew chapter 22."

"That's right," continued Chief, "and what is it we've been looking at in our last couple of studies?"

"The uniqueness of Jesus," replied Abigail, trying to make herself more comfortable on the sofa.

"True," nodded Chief, "but tell me more about that. What about Jesus has proven to be so unique?"

"Well," Abigail started, "he is supposed to be this poorly-educated carpenter's son. And the best educated people in his society are trying to make him look like a fool because of it, but they can't. Jesus has answers to every one of their questions."

"Amazing answers too," Tomas chimed in. "Jesus just seems to know more about God than any of them."

"Duh, it's because Jesus is God," Grace exclaimed.

"Yes," Chief said, smiling at Grace, "we believe that. But we want to take an honest look at the question to see if our belief is reasonable."

"What's reasonable mean?" Grace asked.

"Reasonable means that it really makes sense based on the facts," Declan answered patiently, as he always did with Grace.

"So let's see if believing in Jesus is rea-son-able," Grace declared, emphasizing each of the syllables, "but don't expect me to read this week. I'm tired of all the Fairy Bees and Sadies. Their names are so weird."

Chief chuckled.

"Well, there are more Fairy Bees," he said, "so who else would like to read, beginning in verse thirty-four?"

"I will," Grant replied, to the great surprise of the group. He had never offered to read before.

Chief gave him a big smile and a nod.

"Hearing that Jesus had silence the Sadducees, the Pharisees got together," Grant began in a rich tone. "One of them, an expert in the law, tested him with this question: 'Teacher, which is the greatest commandment in the Law?'"

"Is this another trap?" Miles interrupted, looking to Chief.

"It is. Does anyone know why?"

"I think I do," said Declan. "My dad once told me that the religious leaders would constantly argue about the most important commandments. Apparently, they would try and rank them."

"Absolutely right," Chief said. "Now listen to Jesus' answer."

Grant continued.

"Jesus replied; 'Love the Lord your God with all your heart and with all your soul and with all your mind.' This is the first and greatest commandment. And the second is like it: 'Love your neighbor as yourself.' All the Law and the Prophets hang on these two commandments."

"Spot on," declared Talia after Grant had finished.

"I don't get it," said Grace.

"Can anyone help?" asked Chief. "What's so special about Jesus' answer?"

"How simple and clear it is," Talia explained. "If you really were trying to rank God's commands, you could go on forever and ever, with everyone having an opinion. But look at Jesus' answer. 'Love God. Love your neighbor. The entire Old Testament is built on these two ideas.' Brilliant!"

"I think we all kind of rank God's commands," Miles offered, "whether we realize it or not. For instance, murder ranks higher than saying a bad word, and stealing is worse than lying. But Jesus' answer really does blow it all up. When someone says, 'Love God. Love others,' there really isn't anything left to say. That covers it so perfectly that any list seems silly."

"I think I get it now," Grace said thoughtfully.

"Thousands of words in the Old Testament," said Abigail, "and hundreds of commands. But Jesus sums it all up in two sentences!"

"All the people must have been wondering, 'Who is this guy?'" Tomas remarked.

"Good point, Tomas," Chief said. "Let's keep going, because Jesus seems to have had the same thought."

"While the Pharisees were gathering together, Jesus asked them, 'What do you think about the Christ? Whose son is he?' 'The son of David,' they replied."

"Wait," Grace roared, "I don't get it."

"I've got this one," Abigail proclaimed before Chief could speak. "The Christ was the Messiah. He was the one that all of the Jews were waiting for. So when Jesus asks the Pharisees about it, they say that the Messiah is going to be the son of the Jews most famous king—King David. Right?"

"That's right," echoed Chief, adjusting his bad knee. "But keep reading."

"He said to them, 'How is it then that David, speaking by the Spirit, calls him 'Lord'? For he says, 'The Lord said to my Lord: *Sit at my right hand until I put your enemies under your feet.* If then David calls him 'Lord,' how can he be his son?' No one could say a word in reply, and from that day on no one dared to ask him any more questions."

"I love that ending," Tomas said. "But if I'm honest, I have to quote Grace on this one, 'I don't get it.'"

For a moment no one said a word, each of them re-reading the passage for themselves. Finally, Grant spoke.

"I think Jesus is saying that the Messiah can't simply be a descendant of King David."

"Good answer," smiled Chief. "Why do you say that?"

"Well," Grant replied, scratching his head. "If King David calls the Messiah 'Lord' then David is saying that the Messiah is higher, more important, than himself. But how could any descendant of King David be greater than King David?"

"Especially in a culture like that," added Declan, "where your ancestors were looked on with such reverence."

"So what is Jesus saying?" questioned Chief.

It was again Grant who answered.

"I think he's saying that the Messiah is someone very special…someone from God."

"It seems that way," Chief agreed. "Now, let me ask one final question for tonight. We broke this chapter up over the course of several weeks. But if you read it all at once, all of these interactions between Jesus and the Jewish leaders, what impression does Jesus give?"

"That *he* is the Messiah sent from God" Grant said quietly.

"Yes," Chief exclaimed triumphantly. "Jesus can't be trapped, and he answers their questions in a way that he shouldn't be able to answer them. It's like he has inside knowledge. Then Jesus ends with this, 'The Messiah is more than you think.' And who does Jesus appear to be talking about? Himself."

"And his amazing answers seem to back up his claim," Abigail commented, once again wrapping her hair around her pink pen.

"But Jesus never openly claims to be the Son of God," Miles noted.

"Not here," Chief agreed, "but like we said, he does hint that he is someone special, someone who has been sent directly from God. And if you put that together with Jesus' miracles, his forgiveness of others' sins, and his other words and teachings throughout the Gospels, not to mention the resurrection, you are left with one conclusion…."

"That Jesus *is* the Son of God," Grace declared.

"Exactly," affirmed Chief.

There was excitement and agreement at this verdict from everyone except Zayne. Abigail noticed, and spoke up.

"Zayne, is something wrong?" she asked him. "Don't you agree with our conclusion about Jesus?"

"What, huh," Zayne sputtered, apparently having been lost in his thoughts.

"Oh, no," he continued, "I don't disagree at all. If you put this passage together with everything else we know about him, I can't see any other conclusion than that Jesus is the Son of God who came to die on a cross for our sins."

"Then what's the matter?" wondered Talia. "You seem distracted."

"Yeah, I guess that I am. It's just that Jesus' greatest commandment comment got me thinking."

"About what?" Miles asked.

"Simplicity," replied Zayne, standing to his feet, "and Occam's razor."

"Who's what?" cried Grace, giving Zayne a strange look.

"Occam's razor. William of Ockham was a mid-evil Christian whose principal states that among competing hypotheses, you should select the one with the fewest assumptions."

"What are you getting at?" asked Declan intently.

"Well, think about it like this," Zayne said, beginning to pace. "We have Jaden DeSoto, a convicted thief, who is dying. He sends his mother a note which seems to make reference to some money that he has stashed."

"Money we believe is the rest of the coins DeSoto stole from Javier Diaz's safety deposit box," interjected Tomas.

"Right," continued Zayne. "And with this note is a mysterious list of numbers. So what are the hypotheses? One, the list could be the meaningless gibberish of a sick man having memory problems. Two, the list could be nothing but a coincidence and be about something entirely different than the missing coins. Or three, the list could be some kind of map that leads to the location of the coins. Now, given all of the facts, which hypothesis is the simplest?"

"The third one," concluded Miles, having begun to see what Zayne was getting at.

"Okay," said Abigail, "I agree. The simplest explanation is best. I also think it must be a map. But we can't unlock the code without a key." She thought for a moment. "My bet is that there's a word that's the key."

"What did you say?" Zayne asked Abigail, after stopping dead in his tracks.

"I said, 'I agree that the simplest explanation is best.'"

"No, not that. What was the last thing you said?"

"I said, 'a word is the key,' so what?"

Zayne's eyes grew wide.

"That's it!" he cried. "That's it. *The Word* is the Key, for *that* is the simplest explanation. How could we not have seen it before? It was right there. Jesus even said it to the Sadducees, 'you are in error because you do not know the Scriptures or the power of God.' Well, we made the same mistake."

"What's right there?" begged Abigail. "What are you talking about? Do you know the key?"

"Yes, of course I do. We all do."

"Well, what is it?"

"It's *The Word*."

"What word?" Abigail pleaded, at the end of her patience.

"What do Christians refer to as *The Word?*" Zayne asked as a light danced within his eyes.

"The Bible," Abigail responded, "but I don't see what that has to do with…" However, Abigail didn't finish, for suddenly she saw it too.

"Oh my," she exclaimed, "You're right! It's the most obvious answer. We were fools not to see it earlier."

"What is the most obvious answer?" cried Grace. "Once again, I have no idea what you are all talking about."

"The Word is the key," her sister replied. "Jaden DeSoto's list of numbers is a list of Bible verses!"

Chapter Seventeen

"I see it," said Declan. "It is the most obvious answer. DeSoto said himself that he had become a Christian. He even put Matthew 6:21 in his note to his mother, 'Where your treasure is, there your heart will be also.' It just has to be a treasure map that uses Bible verses."

Abigail, who had seated herself at the folding table with her Bible in front of her, pulled out a copy of DeSoto's list and set it beside her. Everyone quickly gathered around. The list read:

19 2 6 23 6 6 19 60 7 26 42 17 40 7 13 26 42 16 1 35 8

"But how do you figure?" asked Tomas while jockeying to get closer to the front. "It's nothing but numbers."

"Yes," exclaimed Miles, "it is nothing but numbers. Yet what if some of them stand for books."

"What do you mean?" replied Tomas.

"He means," Abigail said, opening her Bible up to the beginning, "that Genesis is book number one."

Tomas' eyes lit up. "Then Exodus is number two, and Leviticus is number three."

"So what's number nineteen?" Talia asked excitedly.

"Nineteen would be Proverbs," answered Zayne. "Wait, no it's Psalms."

Abigail flipped to the book of Psalms as her friends watched anxiously.

"Now what?" she wondered.

"Try Psalm two," replied Talia.

"Oh, I see," Abigail answered, "which means we want…"

But Abigail was interrupted by her little sister.

"Which means we want verse six," cried Grace, who had wiggled her way to the front, just to the right of her sister. "Because the first three numbers are 19, 2, 6. So we want the nineteenth book, the second chapter, and the sixth verse."

"Nice job," Chief said, giving Grace a wink.

"Thanks," Grace replied with a tone of self-satisfaction.

"What does it say?" Miles asked while Abigail scanned the page.

"I have installed my King on Zion, my holy hill," recited Chief unexpectedly.

"That's right," confirmed Abigail. "How did you know?"

"I have that Psalm memorized," Chief answered.

"So what does it mean?" asked Talia, a confused look upon her face.

"I have no idea," replied Declan, "but let's write that down and try the next one."

Tomas quickly retrieved the Case File from where he had left it, on the floor beside Chief's recliner. Then he took a seat at the table next to Abigail. While he copied the verse onto a blank page in the binder, Abigail began flipping pages towards the left.

"Our next number is twenty three," she began. "And if the Psalms are book nineteen then that means Isaiah."

"Try Isaiah chapter six and verse six," proclaimed an excited Grace, who had fully mastered the idea.

"Then one of the seraphs flew to me with a live coal in his hand, which he had taken with tongs from the altar," read Abigail.

"I bet you didn't have that one memorized," Declan said to Chief with a chuckle.

"No," laughed Chief, "you're right about that."

But Miles wasn't laughing.

"Come on," he said dejectedly. "What in the world are these verses supposed to mean? I don't see how this is going to lead to a bunch of hidden coins."

"Don't give up so easily," Talia cautioned. "Let's try another one. Nineteen, sixty, and seven are the next three numbers. That should be psalm sixty, verse seven."

As she spoke, Abigail began turning the pages. When she found the right spot, Abigail read the verse to herself.

She let out a sigh.

"What does it say?" everyone asked.

"Gilead is mine, and Manasseh is mine; Ephraim is my helmet, Judah my scepter," she answered.

"It seems like we have a puzzle within a puzzle," spoke Zayne. "This is no simple treasure map."

"Wait," said Grant. "If this is a treasure map, maybe we are supposed to be taking locations out of these verses. Tomas, read that first verse again."

"I have installed my King on Zion, my holy hill," Tomas read.

"There are only two locations in that verse," Abigail began. "One is Zion and the other is hill."

"Keep in mind Occum's razor," suggested Zayne.

Talia scratched her forehead and then began to speak. "Well," she said, "although there might be something named Zion around here, a hill is a lot simpler."

"Okay," said Declan, "let's assume that hill is what we're looking for. How about reading the next verse again?"

Tomas looked down at his notes.

"Then one of the seraphs flew to me with a live coal in his hand," he read, "which he had taken with tongs from the altar."

"There isn't really a location there, except maybe an altar," indicated Abigail. "Could we be looking for an altar on a hill?"

"Maybe," pondered Declan. "Re-read the third verse."

Abigail, who was still on the proper page in her Bible, did so.

"Gilead is mine, and Manasseh is mine; Ephraim is my helmet, Judah my scepter."

"I don't know," said Miles, "Gilead, Manasseh, Ephraim, and Judah don't seem likely. The only other key words are helmet and scepter, but those aren't locations. However, there isn't really anything else. So we've got hill, altar, and either helmet or scepter. That doesn't mean anything to me."

"Nor to me," echoed Zayne. "But notice. The word 'mine' is repeated in the verse. Perhaps he meant it in another way? Then we'd have hill, altar, and mine?"

"A hill with an altar and a mine," declared Abigail. "I have no idea where that would be, but it is at least a reasonable place to start."

"Come on," chided Grace. "If you are looking for the simplest explanation then get rid of the altar."

"Why?" Abigail protested.

"Because I don't even know what an altar is," Grace answered.

"An altar is just a kind of table," snipped her sister. "There could be an altar on a hill."

"I don't think so," Grace grumbled.

"Then what would be the second word?" Abigail questioned angrily.

"I thought the second word should have been coal," offered Grace. "It is a much simpler word. Everybody knows what coal is."

Abigail rolled her eyes and said, "So our three words would be hill, coal, and mine. I don't…" But after realizing what she had said, Abigail stopped.

"Oh my," she proclaimed. "Is my sister a genius? What if we are looking for a coal mine on a hill? That makes a lot more sense."

"Chief," Declan asked, "is there a coal mine around here?"

Chief thought for a moment.

"I don't think so," he said. "They do some quarrying for rocks in the hills just outside of town, but I don't think they ever did any coal mining there."

"You do have to admit," Tomas offered, "it is the easier explanation. But let's keep going. Maybe the later verses will help."

"The next book is number twenty-six," instructed Talia. "I think that would be…Ezekiel. Try Ezekiel 42:17."

Abigail found the verse. "Get this," she said excitedly, "'He measured the north side; it was five hundred cubits by the measuring rod.' It's a distance—five hundred cubits."

"I'll bet it's a distance and a direction," added Declan. "Five hundred cubits, north. But what's a cubit."

"It was an ancient measure of length," Chief instructed.

"Yes," agreed Zayne. "It was approximately the length of a person's forearm, or about eighteen inches. So, a foot and a half. That would make this twenty-seven feet, plus point seven, seven, seven, seven…."

"We get the idea," Abigail groaned.

"It's just that the decimal repeats," grinned Zayne.

"Wait, Zayne," said Chief, "there were actually two different lengths for the cubit. You're right, the Hebrew length was about eighteen inches. But Ezekiel used the so called royal cubit. It was about twenty inches."

"Oh yes, the royal cubit," Zayne gasped. "I can't believe I didn't think of that. In that case, the distance would be twenty-five feet. In case you are wondering, there are no decimals."

"Zayne," cried Tomas, "how in the world do you know so much about cubits?"

Zayne looked directly at Tomas, and without any expression of humor, said, "I have a cousin named Cubit."

After staring at him in disbelief, Tomas finally replied, "You can't possibly be serious."

From the look on Zayne's face, he was quite serious.

"Come on," Talia said impatiently, "let's read the next clue. The numbers are forty, seven, and thirteen. What would that be?"

Miles, who had been following along in his own Bible, replied, "Matthew 7:13." And having already turned there, he read.

"Enter through the narrow gate, for wide is the gate and broad is the road that leads to destruction, and many enter through it."

"Wow," exclaimed Declan. "After you go the twenty-five feet there must be some kind of gate. What's next?"

"Twenty-six, forty-two, and sixteen," answered Talia.

"That's Ezekiel again," added Miles. "Ezekiel 42:16. One verse before the other."

This time Abigail read.

"He measured the east side with the measuring rod; it was five hundred cubits."

Grace began to jump up and down.

"Go east, twenty-five feet," she cheered. "Only one more clue to go!"

"One, thirty-five, and eight," said Miles. "Genesis 35:8."

Abigail raced to the front of her Bible.

"I've got it," she said excitedly. "Get a load of this. 'Now Deborah, Rebekah's nurse, died and was buried under the oak outside Bethel. So it was named Allon Bakuth.' The coins are buried under an oak tree!"

"Wait," said Declan. "I thought we were inside of a coal mine. How is there an oak tree?"

"Good question," replied Talia. "Maybe it isn't an oak tree. Maybe it's just something made of oak."

"It could be," acknowledged Declan.

"Whatever it is," said Abigail, rising from the table and turning to face her friends, "we'll know when we get there. Because now we are going to get there. We have it! A real treasure map to the location of the stolen coins."

"You are forgetting one thing," cautioned Talia. "We have no idea where to find this coal mine on a hill?"

"Oh, yeah," Abigail replied sadly. "In all the excitement, I forgot about that."

Declan walked away from the table and toward the middle of the room. As he usually did when in deep thought, he began to pace.

After a few short laps, he paused.

"For some reason," Declan began, "I feel like I've seen a mine recently. But I can't place it. And I don't even know how that could be possible. I must be imagining it."

"That's so funny, Declan," Abigail said, "I've been having the same thought. There's this image in my mind of an old tunnel. Yet I haven't been anywhere like that. Maybe it was a show I saw or something."

"That's it," Declan exclaimed. "It's an *image* of an old tunnel."

"Huh?" said Abigail, confused.

"A photograph," clarified Declan. "Don't you remember? A few weeks back, when all of this started, you and I were looking through some of Chief's photo albums."

"But, Chief, don't you mostly just take pictures of flowers?" Grant wondered.

"I do," Chief answered with a light in his eyes, "however...."

Without finishing, Chief hobbled out of the room. In a short time, he returned, carrying a photo album. He placed it on the table and then began turning page after page, quickly scanning the photos as he went. Finally, he let out a triumphant cry.

"Yes," he declared, pointing to a photograph. "Abigail and Declan, you did see a picture of an old tunnel. I took this photo several years ago. The tunnel wasn't the subject. I was interested in these beautiful wildflowers growing nearby, but the tunnel was there, in the background."

"Where were you Chief?" asked Talia passionately.

"Well, I'm not exactly sure. It was a long time ago, and I go all over taking my photos. Wait, I've got an idea. Let me give a quick call to a friend. He's a local historian, and he might know something about it."

Chief went into the kitchen and dialed his friend as the others waited anxiously for the verdict. After about five minutes had passed, the members of the Bible Club could hear Chief say, "Thanks, Bernie, I appreciate it. And, yeah, we'll do that fishing soon. Goodbye."

A moment later, Chief reappeared with a look of triumph on his face.

"My friend said that they did quite a bit of coal mining here in the eighteen-hundreds. But that the quarry company had a small operation back in the sixties. The coal markets dropped and it no longer looked profitable, so they gave up on the idea. After I described the photo, he thinks it has to be a picture of that nineteen sixties shaft. He knew exactly where it was. And I'm sure he must be right. When I've been looking for wildflowers, I've visited that area lots of times. It's just outside of town by the current quarry."

When Chief had finished talking, cheers erupted.

"We've done it," exclaimed Miles. "We've got our coal mine on a hill!"

"So what do we do now?" inquired Abigail.

Chief smiled and then said, "Well, it looks like you're going on a hunt for buried treasure."

Before going home that night, they had decided upon a plan.

The next day, Declan, Abigail, and Grant would explore the hillside on the outskirts of town and find the entrance to the mine. If it looked like they could get in and that it would be safe, the Bible Club would return the following evening to begin searching for the coins. They would also be very careful not to be followed.

The bearded man was out there somewhere, and he was searching for the treasure too!

Chapter Eighteen

By following the directions of Chief's friend Bernie, the scouting trip went perfectly.

The hill in question was on land owned by the quarry company. But it adjoined a wooded area, owned by the county, frequented by both hikers and hunters; and if the two properties had once been separated by fencing, they weren't any longer. So the only obstacle in reaching their destination was a somewhat lengthy walk through the woods.

Upon finding the hill, they discovered the old mine was just where Bernie said it would be, behind a small grove of pines near the hilltop.

Although well hidden by the trees, it was obvious that others had found the place too. Used bottles and cans littered the ground outside the entrance, and several spots had the markings of past campfires. However, none of the activity looked very recent.

At first glance, the mine itself appeared to be sealed up tight. An imposing steel gate barred the entrance, and a heavy metal chain with an enormous lock made sure that the gate remained secure. However, as the three friends soon learned, appearances can be deceiving. Yes, the gate was sealed up tight, but in the bottom right corner of the mine's entryway, several rocks had crumbled away. These missing stones left a gap between the gate and the wall. With a little determination, this gap would allow even a grown man to squeeze his way through.

Following their examination of the gap, the three investigators shown their flashlight down into the opening. What they saw appeared safe enough. And once more, they noticed clear evidence that others had previously been there. More trash lay in the tunnel, and graffiti decorated the walls.

Having now done what they had set out to do, the friends made their way back to town, and to their rendezvous with the rest of the Bible Club.

"Good work," said Chief, after Declan, Abigail, and Grant had finished telling everyone what they had seen.

As the Bible Club turned their attention from their three advance scouts back to their leader, the excitement in Chief's living room had never been higher.

"Okay, I know that you are all ready to go on your treasure hunt," Chief continued, with everyone listened intently, "but there are a few things we need to talk about. First, I was on the phone today with the quarry company. The man I spoke to said that they can't grant us official permission to look in the coal mine without a court order or without sending them a written request. Obviously, we aren't in a position to get a court order unless we hand the entire case over to the police department. And, at present, my friends at the station said that they simply don't have the manpower to help us look for the coins. As for the official request, the man from the quarry said it can take between two weeks to a month to get approval. Of course, we can't wait that long."

"No, we can't," cried Talia. "Our bearded friend might find the coins and be long gone by then."

"True," agreed Chief, "but I'll get back to him in a minute. As for the access, we aren't done for quite yet. The man from the quarry said that he couldn't give us official permission. However, he did say that, unofficially, the quarry company knows that people trespass in the coal mine all the time. They don't like it, but the mine is so small and so safe that they haven't put forth any effort to stop them.

Basically, the mine shaft barely goes anywhere, for the company gave up on the mining idea after just a few months."

"So we can look for the coins?" asked Tomas happily.

"Yes. But," warned Chief, putting out his right hand like a stop sign, "they don't want us going around telling people that we've been in there. Understand?"

Everyone agreed.

"Now as for the bearded man," added Chief, "my friends at the police station have been able to identify the photo. He's a small time crook named Arnie King, and he just got out of prison about a month and a half ago. Apparently, King did three years for holding up a convenient store. But does anyone want to take a guess at who he once had as a cellmate?"

"Jaden DeSoto," responded Zayne casually.

"Right," nodded Chief. "So this guy is not someone we should be messing with. However, I've got good news and bad news. Last night, someone fitting King's description tried to cross the border into Canada using a fake passport."

Miles finished Chief's thought for him.

"So, the good news is that King no longer appears to be a problem," he said. "But, the bad news is that he had some reason to try and escape into Canada."

"Like he already found the coins," said Talia dejectedly.

"I'm afraid it looks that way," Chief concluded. "He didn't have the coins on him, but that doesn't mean he hasn't hidden them or passed them on to someone else."

"I guess our treasure hunt is over before it even started," murmured Tomas.

"Probably," acknowledged Chief. "Yet it's still worth taking a look. I've spoken to all of your parents this morning just to make sure they understand exactly what's going on. And under the circumstances, they all feel comfortable allowing you to explore the cave. Except for you Grace. Your parents felt like Abigail is old enough but that you aren't. Sorry."

"I knew it," Grace fumed. "I never get to explore old mines for buried treasure."

"This has happened to you before?" Tomas asked sarcastically.

Grace gave him a nasty look while the others chuckled.

"Don't feel too bad, Grace," said a disappointed Miles. "I can't very well explore caves either, not in this wheelchair."

"And don't *you* feel too bad, Miles," added Chief. "I'm also not going. My knee has been getting better after the surgery, but there's no way I can go scurrying through an old mine. I don't even think I would be able to climb up the hill."

For the remainder of the evening, plans were finalized for the treasure hunt that would take place the next night. At first, much of the excitement had been stolen by the revelation that Arnie King, Jaden DeSoto's former cellmate, had probably already made off with the coins. Yet by their very nature, treasure hunts have a way of stirring hope even when the odds are the longest. So in spite of themselves, the Bible Club couldn't prevent their sense of enthusiasm from slowly returning. Even Miles and Grace, who were extremely disappointed at first, began to forget their sadness, and by the end of the evening were just as excited as if they were going too.

Soon the Bible Club said their goodnights, and everyone made their way home to their beds. However, with adventure waiting for them the next day, no one got much sleep. No one, that is, except the eccentric redhead, for Zayne slept like a baby.

It was seven o'clock the following evening when Abigail, Declan, Talia, Grant, Tomas, and Zayne made their way through the woods. The late start had been necessary to assure that no one from the quarry was still at work.

They didn't want their treasure hunt to be stopped before it had even begun.

Declan and Grant each carried shovels. Abigail had a heavy metal bucket. Resting upon her right shoulder, Talia brought a small pick axe. In a backpack, Tomas carried water bottles, flashlights, and a paper with the precious clues to the location of the coins. As for Zayne, he trudged along in his froggy boots, carrying only a flashlight. He had been in charge of bringing some gardening trowels, but somewhere along the way, he had already managed to lose them.

"Are we getting close?" asked Talia as she stepped over a fallen tree branch that crossed the path.

"Almost," answered Abigail. "I think we've just entered onto the quarry's property."

"No," corrected Declan. "I think it starts up ahead there. Do you see that post? It looks like a property marker to me."

The friends continued along the path, and the further they went, the more overgrown it became. Finally, the trail ended entirely, and they found themselves out of the woods and standing on a grassy hillside.

From there, Declan, Abigail, and Grant led their friends up the hill, behind the pine trees, and to the mine.

Upon their arrival, everyone needed a quick rest. The journey had been a couple of miles and the children were both tired and thirsty. Tomas passed out the water bottles. But after a drink and a chance to catch their breath, the group felt refreshed. The water bottles were put back in Tomas' backpack, and then they gathered together at the entrance to the mine.

With the sun growing lower in the western sky, Declan volunteered to enter the mine first. The others agreed. So after pushing his shovel through the gap between the gate and the stone wall, he lowered himself to the ground and crawled through on his belly. Once safely inside, Declan got back on his feet. Tomas passed a flashlight to him between the bars of the gate.

Slowly Declan shown the light around him, first on the walls and then on the ground.

"Let me take a quick look before you all come in," he said, disappearing down the corridor.

He returned a moment later.

"Looks good," he offered. "Like Chief said, I don't think safety is going to be an issue. The walls and ceiling are reinforced with concrete and steel. This isn't some rickety, old mine like in the movies."

"Good," Abigail said, visibly relieved. "Let's all go in so we can get started."

One at a time, the treasure hunters passed their supplies through the opening, and then they slid themselves through. Grant, by far the largest member of the group, got temporarily stuck in the gap. However, after some anxious twisting and turning, as well as a few pushes and pulls from his friends, he too safely reached the other side. Finally, while Zayne, the last person to enter, was standing up and brushing himself off, Talia caused the entire group to pause.

"Did you see that?" she whispered.

"What?" Abigail replied nervously.

"Down there," Talia said, "at the bottom of the hill where we came out from the woods. I thought I saw something."

"I thought I saw something too," Tomas confided.

The group barely breathed as they peered through the gate. For several minutes the friends watched, until finally they saw a small animal, perhaps a rabbit or a fox, dart from the woods. Everyone exhaled.

"It was nothing," Declan sighed. "Come on. It's getting late and we promised Chief and Miles that we'd be back at the van by nine-thirty. We don't have that much time."

The friends turned their attention toward Tomas, who had removed the list of clues from his backpack. After pointing his flashlight at the paper, he began.

"Okay, the first three clues are already finished. We are in the coal mine on the hill. So far so good. Now, assuming we are correct, the next clue says to go twenty-five feet north."

Grant pulled a small compass from his pocket and then smiled.

"Yeah," he said, "the tunnel leads north alright."

Tomas removed a tape measure from the backpack's front pouch.

"I don't know how precise we need to be," Tomas said as he placed the metal end of the tape measure on the ground just inside the gate, "but I'll hold this here. Abigail, take the other end and start walking. The next clue is 'enter through the narrow gate.' See what you can find up ahead."

Abigail handed her bucket to Talia. Then with a flashlight in one hand and the tape measure in the other, she walked deeper into the tunnel. Declan and Grant joined her, while Zayne and Talia remained with Tomas.

"That's twenty-five feet," she called out, "but I don't see anything."

Tomas let go of his end of the tape measure and Abigail let it retract. Then Tomas, Zayne and Talia caught up to the others. From where they were standing, the tunnel seemed to go further on in the same northern direction for quite some time. They scanned the walls with their flashlights, hoping for some kind of clue.

"There's nothing here," Talia finally declared.

"Nothing," agreed Declan, "except lots of rock."

However, Zayne was up to something. He started at the spot which marked twenty-five feet and then took several additional paces north. It wasn't much further, but after shinning his flashlight, he noticed something on the eastern wall, something that hadn't been visible previously because of a natural column of rock protruding from the side of the tunnel.

He and the others hurried over to examine.

They had discovered a steel door.

"Nice job, Zayne," cheered Abigail.

"I guess Jaden DeSoto was using the Hebrew cubit instead of the royal cubit," explained Zayne. "He was incorrect in doing so, of course. Chief is right. The book of Ezekiel does suppose the use of the twenty inch cubit."

"Who cares about the size of the cubit?" Tomas said. "At least we found something. But how are we supposed to get through that?" He motioned toward the door. "It looks like the entrance to a bank vault."

"We could try turning the handle," suggested Zayne in all seriousness.

No one could argue with the simplicity of Zayne's suggestion. So Declan stepped forward, turned the rusty handle, and pulled.

To everyone's great surprise, it opened easily.

"Yes," laughed Declan, "I suppose we could just try turning the handle."

With the old door now open, the members of the Bible Club shined their lights down a very narrow side-passage.

"Well, we've found the narrow road," joked Talia. "Tomas, what were we supposed to do next?"

"Go east for another twenty-five feet."

"We had better make that twenty-seven point seven, seven, seven feet," corrected Zayne. "Don't forget. We need to use the Hebrew cubit."

Tomas rolled his eyes, but said nothing. Instead, he took the metal tab of the tape measure from Abigail. Then once again, he kneeled upon the ground, holding it right at the middle of the doorway.

Abigail then began to walk, causing the tape measure to extend as she went.

The passage was indeed narrow, which meant that the others couldn't follow her without interfering with the tape. So Abigail went on her own, and after a few feet, vanished around a small corner.

"Oh no," they heard her cry.

"What's wrong?" asked a worried Talia. "Are you okay?"

"Yes," Abigail answered, a tone of frustration in her voice, "I'm fine. But the passage is a foot deep with water here. My shoes are soaked."

Zayne grinned, winked at the others, and pointed at his rubber boots.

This time, everyone rolled their eyes.

A moment later, Abigail spoke again, her voice somewhat muffled by the stone walls.

"All right, I'm at twenty-eight feet," she declared, "and I'm…I'm…at the entrance to some kind of room. Come on."

After Tomas released the tape measure and it retracted away toward Abigail, the others followed in a single file line. When each of them had gone halfway, they encountered the water that their friend had warned them about. Unfortunately in the narrow passage, there was no way to avoid it, and so everyone now had cold, soggy feet—except Zayne.

Upon reaching Abigail, the tunnel opened up, revealing the room of which she had spoken.

As their flashlights searched the darkness, they appeared to be in a natural cavern of some kind, in contrast to the previous tunnel, which clearly had been man-made. And it was of sizeable dimensions. Zayne estimated it to have a width of about twenty yards and a length of forty. As for the ceiling, he guessed that it reached twenty-five feet. And although very dark, the room was not entirely without light. For at the far end, a bit of dim moonlight shown down from somewhere above. Yet what immediately caught their attention was a strange twisted shape, half in moonlight and half in shadow. What it might be exactly, they could not tell.

"What's that?" wondered Talia, pointing toward the large object with the beam of her flashlight.

Answering Talia's question with a question, Abigail replied, "It couldn't be a tree, could it?"

Declan walked slowly toward the shape, keeping his flashlight fixed upon it.

"That's exactly what it is," he explained. "Apparently, it took hold in the dirt floor, and twisted itself like a pretzel, straining toward that light."

Tomas joined Declan.

"Wow," he then exclaimed, directing his light toward the ceiling, "there must be some kind of natural spring outside. Look, there's a steady trickle of water flowing down from that opening. Then the water forms a small pool here on the ground."

"And then it turns into a little stream which runs all the way back into the tunnel," Abigail added.

"Which is why our socks are all wet," added Declan.

Zayne smiled to himself, but wisely chose not to say anything.

"Did this little stream of water form this entire room?" inquired Talia.

"Probably," Zayne concluded. "And I'll bet you that the miners joined their tunnel into this cavern for a natural air shaft. That hole in the ceiling, joined together with the mine's entrance, would create enough of a draft to ventilate the entire tunnel quite nicely."

"But did you notice how the tree rises all the way up to the light," Grant said. "I bet you could climb your way out of here, if the opening at the top is big enough."

"You might be right," agreed Declan, "but that isn't the most interesting thing about this tree."

"It's not," replied Grant.

"No," offered Declan. "The most interesting thing about this tree is that it's an oak tree."

"Why is that…" started Abigail, before realizing what Declan was getting at.

"Of course," she exclaimed, "the last clue. The coins are buried under an oak tree. This is it. We've found the spot. I just hope we aren't too late."

Talia began searching the ground by the tree with her flashlight.

"But where do we dig?" she asked. "Even if the coins are here, it might take a week to find them."

"Search for an x," joked Declan, "that's always where the treasure is buried in the pirate movies."

"Don't laugh," Abigail said. "Look here!"

While Declan was speaking, Abigail had gone around the back side of the tree to investigate. As she did, the light of her flashlight picked up something unexpected.

"There," she said, illuminating a spot at the base of the oak. "Someone has actually carved an x into the tree. The coins must be over here."

"I don't believe it," exclaimed Declan. "X really does mark the spot."

"And notice the ground," added Tomas. "It's different than everywhere else. Most of the floor is rock, but this looks to be all dirt."

"Well, let's start digging," Abigail said excitedly.

The area between the tree and the cavern wall was small and tight. It only allowed for two diggers at one time. So the friends took turns. And although it didn't require the pick axe, plenty of loose rock in the soil made the work difficult.

Finally, after about twenty minutes, Declan thought he spotted something in the hole.

"Zayne, let me borrow your flashlight. I think I see something."

After kneeling down and examining the ground, Declan found a piece of quartz.

"Shoot, it's nothing," he said.

But as Declan rose and began to hand the flashlight back to Zayne, he stopped.

"Zayne," Declan asked, giving the flashlight a strange look. "What kind of flashlight is this? I've never seen anything like it."

"Oh," answered Zayne, "it's just a stun gun flashlight."

"A what?" Declan cried.

"A stun gun flashlight. Besides being a light, it's also a five million volt stun gun."

"You mean, a stun gun like the police use to electrocute people?" asked a wide-eyed Abigail.

"Electrocute isn't the correct term," explained Zayne. "Electrocution implies serious injury or death. A stun gun does shock people, temporarily disrupting their motor function, but it does not lead to serious injury."

"What are you doing with a stun gun?" Tomas blurted.

"I got it for those experiments with the hamster."

Zayne's companions stared at him angrily.

"Just kidding," laughed Zayne. "I bought it after we had that run in with Arnie King outside of Mrs. DeSoto's house. It's just a safety precaution."

"You mean that you would actually stun King with that?" wondered Talia.

"Absolutely," he said without hesitation.

"Well, just be careful with it," Declan cautioned, handing it back to Zayne. "If you drop that thing in the water, you might fry us all."

"Not me," said Zayne, unable to resist, "my froggy boots are one hundred percent pure rubber, which means that they don't conduct electricity. I'd be safe."

"Nice," Declan groaned. "Just be careful, okay?"

While the others had been discussing Zayne's flashlight, Grant had continued digging. Just then, the sound of metal against metal rung out through the cavern. His shovel had hit something. The others gathered around as Grant examined the hole.

"There's something here," he announced. "It's a metal box. I think it's locked. Wait, no. It isn't. I can get the lid all the way open if I just clear away some more of this dirt."

The others waited breathlessly.

"There. Yes, I think I can open it now."

With all of his strength, Grant pulled at the lid of the strongbox. At first the box resisted, but soon it yielded to his mighty force.

Staring down at his discovery, Grant let out a long whistle.

"What is it? What is it?" Abigail begged, unable to see past Grant's large frame.

"If you want my guess," replied Grant, moving out of the way to show the others the box full of gold and silver. "It's a couple million dollars in rare coins!"

Chapter Nineteen

Miles and Chief sat together in Chief's 1986 custom van, a mainstay on his fishing trips, waiting for the rest of the Bible Club to return.

Almost two hours prior, they had dropped their friends off at a hiking trail that slowly wound its way to the quarry's property. Chief now had the driver's seat reclined, reading a Lord Peter Wimsey mystery novel. And Miles was in the passenger's seat beside him, flipping through the Bible Club's Case File.

As he turned to another page, Miles noticed that Chief was once again rubbing his bad knee.

"Is it still bothering you?" Miles asked.

"Huh?" replied Chief, looking up from his book. "What did you say?"

"Is it still bothering you?" repeated Miles, pointing at Chief's right knee. "You keep rubbing it."

"Oh, am I?" answered Chief. "I didn't realize it. Well, I wouldn't say that it hurts. It's more of a dull ache."

"Didn't the surgery help?"

"Absolutely, it did. But I'm afraid that it's just always going to give me trouble."

"That's too bad," Miles said sympathetically.

For several more minutes, the two fell back into a silence; Chief engrossed in his book, and Miles reviewing the binder. Then Miles saw a page that he hadn't before.

"What's this?" he exclaimed, more to himself than Chief.

Chief stopped reading and glanced over at Miles and the Case File.

"Yeah, that's new," began Chief, setting his book down upon his lap. "It's the report on Arnie King that came down from the border patrol. I gave Tomas a copy to put in the binder."

"That's what I thought it was," said Miles, a look of concern upon his face.

"Is something the matter?" Chief asked, noticing Miles' anxious expression.

"I don't know. Probably not. It's just this part here. Is this saying that King is right-handed?"

Chief leaned over and examined the paragraph in question.

"Yeah," he answered after reading a few lines. "That's the description the agent gave of King. Why?"

Miles scratched his head.

"Well, it does sound exactly like the man who jumped out at Mrs. DeSoto's house, but...."

"But what?"

"I'm sure this is nothing," continued Miles, "but when King jumped out and took the paper from Tomas, he snatched the paper with his left hand."

"So?"

"This says that the man they stopped at the border is right-handed."

Chief returned his chair to an upright position and turned attentively toward Miles.

"So because he grabbed the paper from Tomas with his left hand," Chief reasoned, "you think that King is left-handed. And, because the report says the man they stopped at the border is right-handed, you wonder if they don't really have King."

"Exactly," replied Miles. "Of course, I could be wrong. But if you were to jump out and grab something from someone, wouldn't you use your dominate hand?"

"I would think so," agreed Chief. The old policeman sat in silence for a moment, and then he asked Miles, "are you sure that he took the paper from Tomas with his left hand?"

"I am absolutely sure. I had just swung my chair around to face Tomas, and I was looking directly at him. After King jumped out, his left side faced toward Tomas and his right side faced toward the rest of us, which was the direction of the street. He snatched the paper and didn't need to turn in order to run, however if he had grabbed it with his right, he would have been reaching across his body, and he would have needed to turn."

The van still had an old police radio mounted to the dashboard. Chief picked up its dangling receiver.

"It could be that the report is wrong about the man being right-handed. Or maybe, for some reason, King grabbed the paper with his weak hand. But, I'd feel a lot better if I checked into it. I'm going to touch base with the station. Perhaps there's more info on the man they picked up at the border."

"Base one. Base one," Chief spoke into the microphone, "this is the old Chief. Come in."

"This is base one dispatch," came a crackling voice in reply. "What do you need, Chief?"

"Is this Wilson? Hey, Wilson. I'm sorry to get on the police line, but I may have a serious situation on my hands. Two days ago,

Sgt. Miller gave me a report that said the border police believed that they had picked up a parolee named Arnie King. He was trying to cross over into Canada with a phony passport. Could you see if there is anything new on that in the computer? Again, sorry, but it might be very important."

"Chief," Wilson replied, "you don't need to apologize. If you think it's important then that's good enough for me. Hold on. I'll look it up."

There was a long silence. Finally, the dispatch came back on the line.

"Yeah, Chief. A positive I.D. came down on that a short time ago. Turns out that it wasn't Arnie King who they stopped with the fake passport. It was some drug runner named Hopkins. Apparently, the agents still can't believe the resemblance."

"Thanks Wilson," Chief answered, "that's what I needed to know."

"Is everything okay?" asked the dispatch. "Do you need me to send a squad car out?"

"I'm not sure yet, but I'll call you back if I do. Thanks for your help. Chief out."

Miles looked nervously at the old policeman.

"Does that mean what I think it means?" he asked.

"It means," Chief explained, "that Arnie King is not detained at the Canadian border, and so…."

Miles interrupted. "And so…he might be out there, right now, looking for the coins."

"And," declared Chief, "the Bible Club might be in very serious danger."

The friends were overwhelmed with excitement as they examined the buried treasure. There were many Roman coins, very similar to the tribute penny they had seen at the home of Jess Evers, but there were also many others. In addition, the box held Spanish coins, Greek coins, Egyptian coins, and Italian coins, as well as some they could not recognize. And despite the wide variety of inscriptions, most of the coins had one thing in common—they were made of gold.

Since gold is quite heavy, the Bible Club had to figure out just how they would remove all the coins from the mine. The strongbox was too much for any one person to carry and too awkward for two.

After some deliberation, however, it was decided that they would put as many coins as they could in their pockets. This made for a good start, but it still left a hefty pile. Finally, they agreed to place the remaining coins in Tomas' backpack and allow the strongest member of the group to carry the coins out upon their back. Obviously, it was a unanimous decision about who was the strongest. So they loaded up the rest of the coins and, with a great deal of effort, lifted the bag onto Grant's broad shoulders.

Although the burden slowed him considerably, Grant was able to walk, and he assured the others that he could get the backpack safely out of the cave. And so the friends began to make their exit. First, they returned to the other side of the large cavern. Then, they entered into the small tunnel which had brought them there. Once again, however, it was necessary to form a single file line due to the narrowness of the passage. Therefore, Zayne led the way, followed by Declan, Abigail, Talia, and then Tomas. Grant, with his heavy burden, came last.

The journey through the narrow tunnel would have been uneventful, except for one thing—Zayne was with them. As a result, while they were filing through the passage, Zayne stopped abruptly.

"Wait," he cried, "I've dropped my flashlight."

"Uh, you mean the flashlight with the built in stun gun?" answered Declan.

"Yeah."

"Into the water that we are all standing in," Declan continued.

"Yeah."

"So, we might all be shocked!"

"No," Zayne corrected him. "Remember, I have on my rubber froggy boots. So I'm safe."

"Zayne," Declan scolded, "that isn't funny."

"Sorry," answered Declan's red-headed friend.

The delay continued as Zayne tried to retrieve his flashlight.

"I can't reach it," he said. "It fell behind me, and I can't turn around."

"I see it," replied Declan. "Fortunately, it isn't in the water. I think I can get it."

Declan carefully slid down between the two walls and picked up the flashlight.

"I got it," he said.

"It's too tight here," Zayne stated. "I can't even turn around to look at you. Would you just shine the light toward me? I'll get the flashlight back from you when we get through. But, whatever you do, don't press the red button on the bottom. If you do, it will be a very shocking experience for me."

After all of Zayne's teasing about his dry feet, Declan found the thought of pushing the red button to be very tempting. But his

Christian nature getting the better of him, he shown the light just as Zayne had asked.

However, it wasn't long before Zayne stopped the line again.

"Uh, guys," Zayne said softly.

"What is it now?" complained Declan.

"Uh, we aren't alone."

A moment before, as Zayne cleared the last portion of the tight passage, he was standing at the doorway which would return them to the main tunnel. But there, a few yards ahead of him, amidst the darkness, Zayne could see a tiny red light floating in mid-air. He knew exactly what it was—the burning end of a single cigarette. After he had whispered to his friends, a voice began to speak.

"Why hello again, kids," a deep, hoarse voice called out. "I haven't seen you in a few days. Not since you gave me that little paper outside of DeSoto's place."

The members of the Bible Club froze in their tracks, with everyone but Zayne still crammed inside the narrow passage.

"You know it's funny," the voice continued as the red light of the cigarette dropped to the ground and then was crushed from existence, "I couldn't make nothing of all those numbers. But luckily for me, I didn't have to. You guys keep doing all the hard work for me. All I got to do is follow you around, and sooner or later, it all works out. I really do appreciate your hard work. And from what I heard, you've gone ahead and dug up all those coins for me. Thanks, I appreciate it. Now, all of you just make your way out here. Then you can give me the coins, and everything will work out just fine."

After Arnie King had concluded his speech, what followed was pure instinct.

Despite knowing the only way out of the mine was toward the voice, all of the Bible Club began a hasty retreat back through the narrow tunnel and toward the cavern where they had discovered the coins. Everyone had cleared the tight passage and had begun to run across the cavern when, once again, the voice of the thug caused them all to freeze.

"I wouldn't be running if I were you," King yelled as he emerged from the tunnel, holding Zayne firmly by his collar. "I'd just hate it if something happened to your little red-headed friend here. Now come back over, like good little kiddos, and give me those coins."

Zayne could feel the strength in the man's grip, and he knew that no amount of struggle would get him free. However, instead of panicking, he calmly stated, "Don't worry Declan. I'll be okay. I've got my froggy boots on."

At first, Declan wondered if Zayne had lost his mind. But then a thought struck him.

"Wait. Maybe Zayne is crazy, but he's also a genius. Why did he only call to me? And why is he talking about his froggy boots?"

Then Declan noticed that Zayne and King were standing ankle deep in the stream of water that ran through the tunnel. And then he remembered that he was still holding Zayne's flashlight. And then he noticed the same stream flowed right beside him. And then he understood exactly what Zayne wanted him to do.

Following a quick prayer, he acted.

Dropping down to the ground beside the stream, Declan touched the flashlight against the water and then pressed the red button. An arc of wavy blue-light, like a miniature lightning bolt, leapt from the flashlight. As it hit the water, the arc exploded into a ball of flame. For a second, the entire cavern lit up like noontime.

Everyone watched in disbelief. Everyone, except Arnie King.

For as the cave filled up with the light of the fireball, a wave of incredible electrical current instantly passed through the stream. King, who was still standing in the water, was blown five feet backwards by the force of the electricity. He then slamming against the cave wall and fell, incapacitated, to the ground.

Zayne too had been standing in the water. However, as he had predicted, the rubber boots had insulated him from the shock. He had been completely unharmed.

Although a clever trick, the Bible Club was by no means out of danger. For despite Zayne's freedom, King still lay between them and the only exit. And although stunned, the effect on the crook would only be temporary.

Everyone gathered by the oak tree.

"What do we do now?" exclaimed Talia frantically.

"We climb," said Abigail firmly.

"What?" Talia replied.

"We climb," Abigail said again, this time pointing up the oak. "The tree is strong, and it goes all the way up to the crack in the ceiling. Maybe the opening at the top is large enough for us to escape."

"Maybe it is," Tomas said skeptically, "but maybe it isn't. We can't see the opening. The crack in the ceiling bends away out of sight."

"Do we have many options?" snapped Abigail.

"We could try to fight our way out," offered Tomas. "We still have the tools. Maybe we could hit him with a shovel. Or what about the stun gun?"

"He's really strong," said Zayne. "I'd estimate the odds of us beating him in a fight to be about a hundred to one. And the stun gun only fires once without a new battery. Besides, he has a gun. When the flash occurred, I could see it tucked into the waistline of his pants."

"Let's go," Abigail exclaimed. "We are wasting time. This is the only way."

No one argued further. Instead, they began to climb, one by one, branch by branch, joining the twisted tree on its quest toward the light. Abigail had gone first, followed closely by Tomas and Talia. Next came Zayne and then Declan. Grant, with the heavy burden of the coins in the backpack, struggled at the rear.

When Abigail had reached the ceiling, she shined her flashlight toward the crack.

"It is an opening," she cried. "Not a very big one, but large enough to squeeze through. You have to step off the tree and onto a ledge. From there it's a short climb to the outside. Looks a little dangerous; the rocks in the opening are wet. However, some of the tree branches stretch over. You can use them like a handrail. I'm going to go for it."

"Be careful," Talia warned.

Still holding on to a higher limb with her hands, Abigail stepped off her branch and onto the rocky ledge. Climbing further upward into the crevice, she soon disappeared from sight.

"I did it," Abigail's voice called down to her friends from up above. "I'm outside. It isn't that hard. Come on."

Tomas went next, and he too safely navigated the slippery rocks, making his way to freedom.

"Blimey," said an extremely nervous Talia.

She took a deep breath and stepped over to the ledge. Then, although moving a bit slower than the others had, she too managed her escape.

Next went Zayne and then Declan.

Both managed the passage nimbly, leaving Grant as the only one still inside.

Shinning their lights down for him, Grant labored to the top branch. The step from the tree to the ledge would be far more dangerous for him than it had been for the others, for a tiny leap was necessary, and he had the added weight of the backpack filled with coins.

Like Talia before him, Grant took a deep breath as he gathered his courage and his strength.

But when he began to move his right foot off of the tree branch and onto the ledge, something terrifying occurred—Grant nearly lost his balance. Yet the cause of the near catastrophe wasn't any lack of dexterity on Grant's part. Instead, just as he had begun, a hand had reached up from below and grabbed a hold of his left ankle.

"I'm a very unhappy person right now," Arnie King growled at Grant, giving the boy's ankle an angry squeeze. "That was a really nasty trick back there, and I didn't like it. So, unless you want this to be your last night on earth, I'd seriously recommend that you give me those coins."

Grant didn't respond. Instead, he was busy calculating whether or not he could make one strong move to pull free and then cross over to the ledge.

Realizing Grant's thoughts, King spoke again.

"Don't you even think about it, kid," he hissed. "You ain't getting free, and you ain't getting up that hole. So stop messing around. My name is Arnie King, and I always get what I want. So give me what's mine, kid, or else I'm going to help you meet your maker."

The words of King's threat impacted Grant in a strange way. Instead of fear, Grant felt an overwhelming sense of peace, and he suddenly realized what he had to do.

"Come on, kid. Give me what's mine."

"Okay," Grant replied as he slipped the backpack off his back.

Then, needing all his strength, Grant held the backpack out away from his body...and over King.

Having realized what was coming, the crook wailed, "Wait! No!"

But it was too late, Grant had already released the backpack, allowing it to slam down upon his adversary. Despite having fallen only a short distance, the weight of the bag, aided by the force of gravity, packed a mighty punch. Striking King directly, the crook lost his grip both on Grant and on the tree, and he tumbled from the oak down to the cave floor.

"Give to Caesar what is Caesar's," Grant muttered to himself, as he easily managed the step to the ledge, having now been freed from his burden.

He scaled the rest of the opening without difficulty and soon stood upon the hillside with his friends.

"What happened down there?" Declan asked.

"I'll tell you later," Grant replied. "Let's get out of here."

No one needed any further convincing, and all six of them began to run down the hill.

Yet they didn't get far, for Arnie King was exceptionally strong and incredibly tough. And despite being in severe pain after striking the rocky ground of the cave, King had immediately risen and begun to climb after Grant.

"That's it," King raged, emerging from the opening up onto the hillside, "you kids have had it." Rising painfully to his feet, King removed the revolver from his waistband and pointed it directly at Tomas, who had only managed to flee about twenty yards.

In his immense anger, it is quite possible that King would have fired the gun, but he never got the chance. For out of the darkness, a single shot rang out, striking King directly in the hand. King's gun went flying, and he let out a flurry of curse words.

Then from the shadows, limping horribly, a sweaty and grimacing Chief emerged.

"Get on the ground, now," the old policeman ordered, "and put your hands behind your back. Declan, take these cuffs and put them firmly on his wrists."

Still cursing in pain, with his hand bleeding profusely, King had no choice but to comply.

"Arnie King," Chief began while Declan secured the handcuffs to the criminal, "you have the right to remain silent...."

Chapter Twenty

As anyone might expect, when people heard that a group of children solved a twenty-year old mystery, found a valuable trove of long-lost coins, and managed to capture a criminal, there was a great deal of commotion. In fact, things were so crazy that the Bible Club couldn't meet together for over two weeks.

During that time, a great number of exciting things occurred.

First of all, the young investigators were interviewed by a number of reporters. To her great delight, even Grace had her moment in the sun. Although, when interviewed, she kept accidently referring to Arnie King as Harry King. (Zayne suspected King's hairy beard as the cause of the young girl's confusion.) Furthermore, each member of the Bible Club had to make an official police statement. Thankfully, this process became much easier after Chief temporarily "un-retired" in order to handle all the details of the case.

However, the most exciting thing caught everyone off guard.

After confirming that the coins had indeed been from the stolen collection of Javier Diaz, a famous British insurance company, named *Heath's*, contacted the police.

Apparently, the firm had long since paid off a claim to the Diaz family for the full value of the stolen goods. So now that the coins had been recovered, this meant that *Heath's* became the rightful owner of the treasure. (And although their rights legally included Jess Evers' tribute penny, *Heath's* decided that the famed actor could keep his prized coin.)

All in all, it worked out quite well for *Heath's*.

The original pay-out for the insurance claim had been one million, two hundred fifty thousand dollars. However, since that time, the value of the coins had more than tripled. As such, *Heath's* Chief Executive Officer, Oliver Heath IV, was feeling quite generous and gave the Bible Club a reward of one hundred thousand dollars.

But *Heath's* was not alone.

Hearing about the case on television, and grateful that it had finally been solved, Javier Diaz's son also wanted to express his gratitude.

Displaying a bit of humor, the business tycoon had a gumball machine, filled with gold colored gumballs, sent to the home of each member of the Bible Club. The boxes included a personalized thank you note as well as a check for one thousand dollars. In the note, Diaz explained how much the coin collection had meant to his father. He also said that he hoped to repurchase the coins from *Heath's* when they were put up for auction, which the insurance company most certainly planned to do. Finally, Diaz extended an invitation for the children to come and visit him, should they ever travel to Mexico.

As for Arnie King, things hadn't been going quite as well.

Following his arrest, King had been taken to the hospital, where besides the bullet wound to his hand, and the dozens of severe cuts and bruises all over his body, it was discovered that he had broken his collarbone after falling from the oak tree. Yet King's worst injury was not physical but psychological. He simply couldn't get over being outsmarted by a bunch of kids. His swollen black eye, which he had received when Grant dropped the backpack on him, serving as a constant reminder.

Yet although things were bad for King, they were about to get much worse.

In addition to a dozen new charges being filed against him, King's actions had violated his parole. So after the hospital, his next stop would be back to federal prison, where he would be staying for, at least, the next twenty years.

On the day Chief handed the convict over to federal custody, the old policeman swore he heard King muttering to himself, repeating the same two words over and over again. The two words were "froggy boots."

"Chief," Abigail began as she and the rest of the Bible Club were taking their familiar places in the living room, "before we start the study, could we talk for a moment? There are still a few things I haven't been able to find out. Everything has just been so crazy."

"Spot on," echoed Talia. "Also, don't forget, Abigail. We have something we need to tell Chief."

"Yes, right," Abigail nodded, "I haven't forgotten."

"Of course we can," Chief said, settling into his recliner. "It seems like forever since we all sat down together."

"I guess being famous isn't as easy as it looks," Grace proclaimed.

"No Grace," Chief chuckled, "I suppose it isn't."

"One thing I've wondered," Abigail said, "was how you showed up just in time? If you hadn't been there, I don't know what would have happened."

"Well, Abigail," answered Chief, pointing over at Miles, "the person you have to thank is right there. If it weren't for him, things might have turned out much differently."

The group looked to Miles for an explanation.

"Uh, well," he started, suddenly feeling his cheeks flush, "while Chief and I were waiting in the van, I was looking through the Case File. Tomas had added a copy of the border police report describing the man they had in custody. It said that he was right-handed. But I remembered that when King stole the paper from

Tomas, he had grabbed it with his left hand. And it just seemed to me, in a moment like that, a person would use their dominant hand."

"So you thought King must be left-handed," Declan stated with a thoughtful look. "Which would mean that the man at the border wasn't King."

"Exactly," confirmed Miles.

Chief picked up the story from there.

"It was a great catch," the old policeman said. "And so, I called into the station to see if anything new had turned up. Well, something definitely had. The border police had discovered that despite the similarities in appearance, they had someone else entirely."

"Chief was amazing," Miles jumped in. "He grabbed a gun out of the glovebox, hopped out of the van, and disappeared into the woods."

"But what about your bad knee?" wondered Talia, staring admiringly at their leader.

"To tell the truth, making it through those woods and up that hill wasn't easy," Chief acknowledged, "but what choice did I have? My family was in trouble."

"I've noticed you're wearing the big brace again," Tomas said. "You reinjured your knee coming to save us, didn't you?"

Chief didn't answer, but his silence spoke volumes.

"Well, you were really something that night, Chief," declared Talia. "I can't believe you blasted that gun right out of King's hand. What an amazing shot!"

Trying to hold back his laughter, Chief explained that it was an amazing shot, but not the one he intended to make. For in truth, he hadn't been trying to hit King in the hand at all.

"I guess my aim isn't what it used to be," he concluded jovially.

"You mean, you were trying to…," Declan didn't finish his sentence.

"Let's just say in a situation like that a policeman isn't trained to aim for someone's hand."

"Wow," Declan replied.

"Now," said Chief, "I've heard everyone's official report on what happened in the mine, and I have to say you were all incredibly brave. You climbed out that tree. Grant dropped the backpack on King's head." Chief grinned. "And then there was Declan and Zayne's little electrical experiment."

"That was all Zayne," Declan proclaimed. "He thought of it. I just did what he told me to do."

"Maybe," Zayne said, genuinely trying to deflect the credit, "but you had to figure out what I meant. And I don't know if I would have had the courage to actually do it. You were awesome."

"Thanks," smiled Declan.

"Let's get back to Grant and that backpack," said Abigail in amazement. "I can't believe you dropped the coins on him like that. What made you do it?"

The shy Grant looked uncomfortable as all eyes turned to him.

"Honestly, the question isn't 'what made me do it,' but rather 'whom made me do it,'" he said softly. There was a long pause before he continued. "Which is kind of what I wanted to tell everyone tonight." His voice now growing stronger. "Because I don't say a whole lot, most of you may not know, but my family aren't Christians. And, until two weeks ago, I wasn't either."

His words were met with surprise.

"I think I wanted to be. I think I believed. But I just couldn't bring myself to fully commit to Jesus. It would mean that I would have to make him the leader of my life, and I just couldn't do it. You see, I'm a really good athlete."

"Uh, that's an understatement," interrupted Tomas.

"Well, and, there are a lot of expectations that come with that, from lots of people that I care about." Grant's voice quivered momentarily, and he paused in order to get his emotions back under control. "So, you see, if I chose to let Jesus be the leader of my life then he might have a different set of expectations for me. And, well, following him might mean that I let those other people down."

Kind and encouraging looks came back at him from all around the circle.

"However," Grant continued, "as we were trying to get out of that cavern, and King grabbed my leg and threatened me, I suddenly realized two things. First, that life really is fragile. And just because I'm young, it doesn't mean that something can't happen to me. Second, I realized that, to be honest, I hate all those expectations that I carry. So why was I holding on to them and allowing them to keep me from becoming a follower of Jesus? And, well, I guess the coins became kind of symbolic. In that one moment, I let go of the burden that was keeping me from getting out of the cave *and* the burden that was keeping me from Jesus."

"You gave to Caesar what is Caesar's," grinned Talia, "and to God what is God's."

"Exactly," smiled Grant.

The room exploded with cheers at the news that Grant had decided to become a Christian, and all of the girls rushed over to give him a hug. Following the hugs, Miles and Grant exchanged a long handshake.

"Wait, wait, wait," Grace shrieked as the commotion died down. "Don't you remember what you all told me when we first studied that verse? You told me that Caesar was like a king. Well, the bad guy's name was Harry King. So…Grant really did give the King what was coming to him."

"He sure did," laughed Abigail, "but his name isn't Harry King. It's Arnie King."

"Oh yeah," Grace frowned. "I keep forgetting that. I don't know why."

Zayne gestured like he was rubbing a long, flowing beard.

Grace stared at him with a look of profound confusion on her face.

As the Bible Club began settling back into their seats, Chief spoke.

"Does that fill in all the blanks now, Abigail?"

"It does," Abigail answered, "but we've still got something we want to tell you. We have decided…."

Abigail paused and looked around the circle at all her friends.

"We have decided," she repeated, "to give the hundred thousand dollars to Alex Townsend."

"Wow," exclaimed Chief, "are you serious? What brought you to that decision?"

"Chief, Alex found the coin," replied Talia. "And without him there wouldn't have been a mystery for us to solve."

"Yeah," agreed Miles, "and besides. He was supposed to use the money from that first coin to go to college. But, with his dad being so sick, his mom had to sell the coin just to try and make ends meet."

"And he's trying so hard to save up for college, driving that bus," Tomas added. "So we want to give him the money. We all think the reward should be his."

"Does everyone feel this way?" Chief asked, deeply impressed by their generosity.

Everyone nodded.

"We talked it over," said Declan, "and we think it's what Jesus would want us to do."

"Well, then I'll make sure that it happens," Chief grinned, immensely proud of his young friends.

"But we are all keeping the thousand dollar reward from Mr. Diaz," smiled Abigail.

"And the gumball machines," Zayne proclaimed, jumping up from his seat.

"By the way, does anyone have any more gold gumballs they can give me?" he asked as he made his way over to a coat closet near the hallway. "I've used all of mine."

"All of them?" Abigail asked in bewilderment. "That must have been nearly two hundred gumballs. We've only had the machines for a few days. How in the world did you chew all of them already?"

"I didn't chew them. I chopped the gum into tiny pieces and used them in my fish experiment," Zayne explained as he opened the closet. "I wanted to see how their swimming would be effected if the water was filled with an elastic polymer."

"You used all two hundred gumballs for an experiment with your fish!" sighed Talia.

"Wait," said Declan cautiously, "you don't have any fish."

"I know," Zayne answered, while removing eight boxes from the closet, each covered in birthday wrapping paper. "I still don't. I went down to the seafood restaurant. They've got that huge tank full of fish when you first come in."

"You filled up their tank with gum!" snapped Abigail. "You didn't!?!"

"No one noticed," Zayne replied calmly, handing one box to each member of the Bible Club. "At least, not at first. Anyway, like I said to the manager, the fish really seemed to like it."

The Bible Club remained in stunned silence as Zayne finished passing out the boxes.

"I'm sorry they are covered in birthday wrapping paper," Zayne explained. "It was all I could find in Abigail's closet."

"I thought that paper looked familiar," said an exasperated Abigail.

"Yeah, thanks for letting me use it."

"I didn't."

"Anyway," Zayne said excitedly, "I went ahead and used some of my thousand dollar reward from Mr. Diaz to get you all a little something. But don't worry, I didn't waste my money. I got you all something very practical. Go ahead and open them."

Unsure what might be inside a present from Zayne, everyone unwrapped their packages with some apprehension.

"Rubber boots?" asked a bewildered Talia.

"Yeah, I got everyone a pair," explained Zayne. "But not just any kind of rubber boots. They're froggy boots." His friends stared at him with blank expressions. "Don't you see? Now all of us have some. So the next time that we're in a similar situation, we will all be safe."

"You mean if we're all ever trapped by an evil criminal in an old coal mine," said Abigail.

"And, we happen to all be standing in water," said Declan.

"And, if we have a stun gun flashlight," said Tomas.

"Then we can shock him, and we'll all be safe," said Talia.

"Precisely," replied Zayne, oblivious to their sarcasm.

Like usual, Zayne's friends could only shake their heads.

"Thanks for the boots, Zayne," Chief offered genuinely, as he began to take off his shoes and place the gift upon his feet.

Seeing Chief's gracious response, the rest of the Bible Club followed his lead. And soon, nine people, and eighteen rubber froggy faces, were all standing together in a circle.

It was an absurd sight which caused them all to laugh merrily.

When the laughter finally died down and everyone had returned once more to their seats, Chief began.

"Well, since your first official case is closed, and it was a smashing success, let's get back to what brought us all together in the first place." Everyone smiled and nodded. "Go ahead and open up your Bibles to tonight's scripture. It's John 4:13-14. But, before we do, who would like to start us off with a prayer?"

"I would," declared Grace quickly and enthusiastically.

"Close your eyes everybody," began the youngest member of the Bible Club. "And no peaking."

They all closed their eyes.

"Dear God," she prayed. "Thank you for Jesus. Thank you for sending him to die on a cross for our sins. And thank you for Grant choosing to follow you. I also pray that Harry King..."

"Arnie King," her sister whispered.

"That's right, Arnie King," Grace acknowledged. "I don't know why I keep calling him Harry."

While keeping his eyes tightly closed, Zayne once again gestured like he was rubbing a long beard. Grace didn't notice. Instead, she resumed her prayer.

"Anyway, God help him to stop doing bad things. And I hope that he will soon become your follower too."

Chief couldn't resist another smile.

"Oh yeah," Grace added. "And thank you for our recent adventure. We just can't wait to see what mystery you have in store for us next. In Jesus' name. Amen."